ALL'S FAIR IN LOVE AND MONEY

SCARBOROUGH FAIR

As realised by SJ Hills

A new twist on an old classic.

A bene placito

Written in a faithful period style and reintroducing the famous trio of the vain fop, the philandering husband, and his long-suffering, adorable wife.

This Work First Published In 2010
by Century17 Publishing, London.
www.century-17.com

This paperback edition first published in 2010

Typeset in Times New Roman by Century17 Publishing.

All rights reserved.
© Copyright, S J Hills, 2010

This book is sold subject to the condition that it shall not, by way of trade or otherwise, be lent, resold, hired out or otherwise circulated without the publisher's prior consent in any form of binding or cover other than that in which it is published, and without a subsequent condition including this condition being imposed on the subsequent purchaser.

First Edition. A-CCVIII
ISBN 978-0-9559921-1-7

Cover artwork by the author, © Copyright 2009

Century17 Publishing
Restoring classics from the past
Rewriting classics for the future

Preface

A new twist on an old favourite. *Scarborough Fair* is a brand new drama based lightly on the classic restoration comedy *The Relapse* by *Vanbrugh (1697)*. It has a different beginning, a different ending, and in order to keep a balance, a different middle, yet still succeeds in paying respectful homage throughout to the original classic work. The result is a delightful romp through the weaknesses and foibles of the upper social classes as they set about finding entertainment for themselves in Scarborough, miles from the civilization which is London.

Written in an eloquent and witty style, with flowing action and wonderful character observation, *Scarborough Fair* picks up the story of the adventuring Tom, as he returns to England flat broke. His brother, Lord Frontbotham, (pronounced Fro'tham), is marrying the young Miss Helen, sight unseen, having heard she is worth a good few thousand a year in income. When Tom's vain, pompous, elder brother turns him down for a small loan, Tom hatches a plan to marry Miss Helen in his brother's place and claim her inheritance for himself.

Mr Lovelace, in Scarborough for the wedding, has fallen suddenly and madly in love with a beautiful young widow seen at a distance in the theatre. When Colonel Cholmondeley discovers the widow he has been pursuing is secretly meeting his good friend, Mr Lovelace, he decides to do the only decent thing: he attempts to seduce Mr Lovelace's lovely wife, Amanda.

Planning a final fling before his wedding day, Lord Frontbotham also pursues the lovely Amanda, declaring, "*she is a condescending woman of such irritating good virtue, I felt it my duty to corrupt her*".

Taking advantage of the complicated trysts evolving in Scarborough, Tom visits Miss Helen pretending to be his elder brother. All is going to plan until the real Lord Frontbotham turns up unexpectedly.

"*With wit and wry humour worthy of the great masters, SJ Hills' works are set to go down as modern classics in their own right. If you get a chance, beg, borrow, or if all else fails even purchase a copy.*"

The language used in this drama is suitable for any period from 1670 to 1930. Latter day expressions and idioms have been carefully avoided, and all wording would have been valid in the 17th century and not out of place in the early 20th. The customs, fashions and settings are also applicable for all inclusive dates.

SJ Hills' works have been described as "*a cross between Wilde and Blackadder*". Rather taken by this, he likes to quote it as often as possible.

"*A witty and amusing observation upon sea, sex and the social consequences, cleverly avoiding the trap of descending into farce*"

Titles by SJ Hills

Scarborough Fair.
Restoration Comedy style drama lightly based upon *The Relapse* by Vanbrugh, considered too risqué to be performed for over 200 years. A witty and amusing observation upon sea, sex and the social consequences.

To Take A Wife.
Restoration Comedy style drama based on *The Country Wife* by Wycherley – famously banned from print for almost 200 years and once considered too outrageous to be performed at all. Now rewritten in SJ Hills' inimitable style.

Wishing Well.
Restoration Comedy style drama, this wonderful play by SJ Hills has a fine balance of bar-room bawdiness, delicious satire and biting wit.

Love In A Nunnery.
Based in 19th Century Italy, this Restoration Comedy style drama contains humour, bawdiness, cunning, scheming, wit, and social comment with a serious underlying theme still just as relevant today. Can the power of love overcome all obstacles?

Greatest Tales of the World. Vol. 1
Classic stories from around the world dramatised for Encyclopaedia Britannica.

Greatest Tales of the World. Vol. 2
More classic stories dramatised for Encyclopaedia Britannica by SJ Hills.

The Star Crossed Lovers.
Romeo and Juliet faithfully translated line-by-line for modern audiences and education.

She Who Would Be King.
Macbeth faithfully translated line-by-line for modern audiences and education.

Love's Last Stand.
Mr Lovelace has been away ten years, dividing his time between brothel and bottle. Returning to London penniless he no longer recognizes his wife, Amanda, who now has the trappings of wealth after a hefty inheritance. Acting the part of a high-class lady of the night, Amanda entices Mr Lovelace into her luxurious house and treats him to the night of his dreams, not revealing her true identity, or the secret she has to impart, until the following morning.

For further titles and information visit www.century-17.com

Contents

Preface		3
Contents		5
Cast List		7

Act I

Act I Scene I.	A Coastal Hotel In Scarborough	11
Act I Scene II.	An Hotel Room	15
Act I Scene III.	The Hotel After A Hearty Meal	20
Act I Scene IV.	Lord Frontbotham's Lodgings	24

Act II

Act II Scene I.	Lovelace's Lodgings. The Drawing Room	38

Act III

Act III Scene I.	Lord Frontbotham's Lodgings, Next Day	56
Act III Scene II.	Lovelace's Lodgings.	62

	Intermission	70

Act IV

Act IV Scene I.	Outside Muddy Moat Hall	71
Act IV Scene II.	A Bedchamber In Muddy Moat Hall	75
Act IV Scene III.	Lovelace's Lodgings	81
Act IV Scene IV.	A Room In Muddy Moat Hall	77
Act IV Scene V.	Sophia's Dressing Room	81

Act V

Act V Scene I.	That Evening In Lovelace's Lodgings	95
Act V Scene II.	That Evening In Muddy Moat Hall	102

	The End	120

Cast List
in order of social standing

Lord Frontbotham
(Pronounced Fro'tham)
Aristocratic vain fool

Sir Tobias Coombs
Country magistrate
Wealthy businessman.
Widower, father of Helen.

Colonel Cholmondeley
(Pronounced Chumley)
A bachelor with an eye for the ladies.

Mr Lovelace
Married gentleman with a roving eye

Tom Frontbotham
(Prefers the alias 'Fashion')
Normal sort of chap.

Johnson
Weary assistant to Tom Frontbotham

Amanda
Faithful and attractive lady
Wife of Mr Lovelace

Sophia
Cunning attractive widow
Cousin to Amanda

Miss Helen
Young and innocent girl
Daughter of Sir Tobias

Nurse
Miss Helen's nursemaid (surprisingly bawdy for such a role)

Dame Cummins
Matchmaker
Spinster of the Parish.

Delaflote
French attendant to Lord Frontbotham

Cast List Continued.

Dr Salomon — Jewish Surgeon

Mr Tailor — Haberdasher

Seamstress — Dressmaker

Tummous — Head of staff at Muddy Moat Hall

Desk Clerk — English wry hotel receptionist

Withers — Butler at Lovelace's lodgings

Porter — Hotel porter.

CAST LIST SPECIAL EDITION

Limited edition to commemorate the first publication of Scarborough Fair – collectors cards to cut-out and play your own seaside charades. Endless fun on a rainy afternoon. Collect them all.
Download in full colour from www.century-17.com

SCARBOROUGH FAIR
As realized by Mr S. J. Hills

ACT I

ACT I SCENE I. A COASTAL HOTEL IN SCARBOROUGH

Scarborough is a seaside resort on the east coast of England,
200 miles from London. The first scene is set in the hotel foyer.

[**TOM** AND **JOHNSON** ENTER THE HOTEL FOYER AND APPROACH THE RECEPTION DESK. THEY ARE DRESSED IN GOOD QUALITY TRAVELING APPAREL FROM A PERIOD OF YOUR CHOOSING, BUT PROBABLY NO LATER THAN 1930, AND HAVE BY ALL APPEARANCES ENDURED A LONG, TIRING JOURNEY. APPEARANCES, HOWEVER, CAN BE DECEPTIVE, THEY ARE FLAT BROKE.]

[UNDER THE FOLLOWING CONVERSATION A PORTER STRUGGLES IN WITH A LARGE HEAVY CHEST BEHIND THE TWO TRAVELLERS. STAMPED IN LARGE LETTERS ON THE CHEST IS THE NAME; '*T. M. FRONTBOTHAM*']

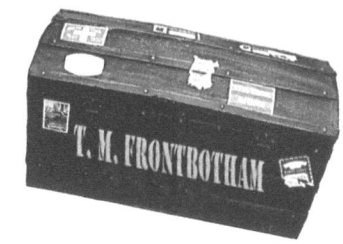

DESK CLERK / (*dry*) Good afternoon, sirs. Welcome to Scarborough. Do you have reservations?

TOM / Indeed I hope so, sir. T. M. Fashion's the name and my assistant here, Mr Johnson.

DESK CLERK / Timmy Fashion. Now let's see...

TOM / Not Timmy! T. M. - T for Thomas, M for Mathias.

DESK CLERK / Ah yes. Lord Front-bottom's younger brother. Welcome, sir.

TOM / It's pronounced 'Fro'tham'.

DESK CLERK / What is?

TOM / (*sighing*) My brother, sir. Lord Fro'tham.

DESK CLERK / (*looking up*) But it's spelt Front...

TOM / (*interrupting*) ...Yes, yes. I know how it's spelt, why do you think I use the name Fashion?

DESK CLERK / I see. And how would you be spelling that, sir?

TOM / F – A – S – H – I – O – N of course. How else would it be spelt?

DESK CLERK / (*dry sarcasm*) I couldn't possibly imagine, sir.

TOM / So you know my brother?

DESK CLERK / By sight only, sir. But then it is quite difficult not to notice him around town, sir.

TOM / Indeed, true words indeed. You'll be glad to hear, I am sure, that the only thing we share in common is our parentage.
(*low, but audible to all*) Though I wonder about that sometimes.

Act I Scene I. The Hotel Foyer

DESK CLERK / (*uninterested, filling in paperwork*) As you say, sir. If you would be so good as to sign here, sir.

TOM / Ah, yes. Right.

DESK CLERK / Will you be settling your account upon your leaving us, sir?

[THE **PORTER** DROPS THE HEAVY CHEST ON THE FLOOR BEHIND **TOM** AND **JOHNSON**.
THE LOUD SOUND REVERBERATES IN THE FOYER]

TOM / (*jumps, and then answers a little over enthusiastically in a high strained voice before falling back into stride*)
Indeed we will, sir, and if my stay in Scarborough is as successful as I plan it to be, there will be healthy reward all round for the fine hospitality I am sure we will be spoilt with during our stay in your wonderful establishment.

DESK CLERK / (*immediately more cheerful*) Then may I be the first to wish you, sir, every success in your endeavours here in our lovely seaside resort.

[**CLERK** PUTS KEY BACK AND TAKES KEY WITH BIGGER FOB FROM THE WALL]

DESK CLERK / Perhaps sir would be happier with one of our finer sea view rooms.
Better air you know.

TOM / Your kindness will not be overlooked I assure you, sir. (*furtively*) I take it there is only a small extra charge for the room?

DESK CLERK / Leave it to me, sir.
(*he taps his nose*) Small change, nothing more.

TOM / Better and better. You know, I am liking Scarborough already. In fact, I am liking it very much indeed. I have good feelings about my stay here. What do you think, Johnson?

JOHNSON / I think we should get our room before it gets too late.

TOM / Too late? It's still early. Too late for what?

JOHNSON / Oh, nothing, sir. Just that it has been a long journey and you probably need to lay down and plan (*out the side of his mouth*) how to spend even more of your money!

TOM / Hmm. Perhaps you are right.
Porter! Our trunk if you please.

[***TOM* AND *JOHNSON* EXIT**]

[THE **PORTER** STRAINS TO LIFT THE TRUNK]

DESK CLERK / (*to porter, dropping into local accent*) It must be som'at they put in t'water in that London. That's second one this week with a name spelled daft. Colonel 'Chowl-mon-der-ly'. Reckons it's 'Chumley'. (*laughs*) Chumley my arse!

ACT I SCENE II. AN HOTEL ROOM

[*TOM* AND *JOHNSON* ENTER THE ROOM. THE *PORTER* FOLLOWS STRUGGLING UNDER THE WEIGHT OF THE TRUNK WHICH HE PLACES HEAVILY ON THE FLOOR AND STANDS WAITING]

TOM / Johnson, pay the porter. (*going to the window*) Not what I would call a sea view.

JOHNSON / (*low to Tom*) Sir, perhaps we should just let the porter take the trunk as payment.

TOM / (*low to Johnson, shocked*) What? Is that all we have left?

[*JOHNSON* NODS HIS HEAD]

TOM / (*Aloud to the porter, thinking on his feet*) You man. What is customary?

PORTER / Just small change, sir.

TOM / Johnson?

[*JOHNSON* RUMMAGES IN HIS POCKET, FINDS A COIN AND HANDS IT TO THE PORTER]

JOHNSON / It's all the small change I have.

PORTER / A whole farthing?! Damn near broke my back that did.

JOHNSON / (*ushering out the porter forcefully*) Yes, yes, thank you. Goodbye.

PORTER / (*disgusted, muttering under his breath*) Town's people. Pah! Nearly broke my bloody back…

[DOOR SLAMS CUTTING SHORT THE *PORTER*]

TOM / Is there nothing left in the trunk, Johnson?

Scarborough Fair (All's Fair In Love And Money)

JOHNSON / Not a thing, sir! The last of your possessions fed us at Selby. Another 20 miles and our next meal would have cost us the coat on your back.

TOM / By heavens! But it appears so heavy, I assumed it must be full.

JOHNSON / I took the liberty of filling it with old newspapers, a farthing a bundle as tall as a gentleman's lounging slacks. Exceptional value for money pound for pound, or rather farthing for ounce I think you'll agree, sir.

TOM / What do I want with old newspapers, Johnson, exceptional value for money or not?

JOHNSON / One must keep up appearances, sir. One couldn't be seen travelling without one's belongings. That would be most unacceptable.

TOM / (*removing his overcoat*) What the devil should I do?

[KNOCK ON DOOR. **JOHNSON** OPENS IT. **DESK CLERK** STEPS IN]

JOHNSON / (*to Clerk*) Ah, just the man. Come to supply the sea view you promised my master. Now that is service.

DESK CLERK / (*humbly*) Sir, the driver is awaiting payment downstairs.

JOHNSON / Ah.

TOM / Well? What is it?

JOHNSON / (*to Tom*) The driver needs paying, sir.

[***JOHNSON*** WALKS BACK INTO THE ROOM TO TAKE ***TOM'S*** COAT LEAVING THE ***DESK CLERK*** AT THE DOOR]

TOM / You there! What's the charge?

DESK CLERK / It's thirteen shillings, sir.

TOM / Right. Do you have change for a guinea?

Act I Scene II. An Hotel Room

DESK CLERK / I do, sir.

JOHNSON / (*to self*) This should prove interesting.

TOM / (*to self*) Now what am I to do?
(*aloud*) Now where did I pack my purse? Have you seen it, Johnson?

JOHNSON / (*after quite a pause while he hangs up the coat*) Shouldn't the man be paid at the desk, sir?

TOM / (*Pointing at Johnson as if he is a saviour and shouting triumphantly*) Yes!

DESK CLERK / Eh?

TOM / (*regaining composure*) As you say, Johnson, I believe that would be proper.

JOHNSON / Yes, sir.

[*JOHNSON* GOES TO THE DOOR AND HOLDS IT OPEN, HIS OTHER HAND ON THE *CLERK'S* SHOULDER]

JOHNSON / Be so good as to arrange for the desk to reimburse the fare, my good man. Put it on our account.

DESK CLERK / Oh, right you are, sir. (*over Johnson's shoulder loud to Tom*) Don't forget a drink for the coachman, sir.

TOM / Yes, yes. The coachman too.

DESK CLERK / Half a crown, sir?.

JOHNSON / (*ushering the driver out the room*) Yes, yes. My master doesn't care what you charge, now be off with you.

DESK CLERK / (*over his own shoulder as he is ushered to the door*) And there's the doorman, sir.

JOHNSON / The doorman?

DESK CLERK / Just small change, sir.

JOHNSON / Damn the doorman. What did he do? You are imposing on a gentleman's generosity now!

[HE SLAMS DOOR IN THE **DESK CLERK**'S FACE]

JOHNSON / Damn cheek of the man, so ready with his change for a guinea.

TOM / By heavens, Johnson. He damn near exposed me.

JOHNSON / So it comes to this. Here we are in Scarborough, not worth a guinea, now you can truly say your cares in the world are over.

TOM / What do you mean?

JOHNSON / I mean, sir, you have nothing left in the world to take care of.

TOM / I still have myself and you to take care of.

JOHNSON / Sir, perhaps if you burdened someone else with that task we would both fare better. Talking of which, about your elder brother, Lord Fro'tham…

TOM / Damn my elder brother.

JOHNSON / With all my heart, but first you must persuade him to provide you with an allowance. You either beg him on bended knee or starve.

TOM / Never in a million years! I will neither beg nor will I starve.

JOHNSON / What will you do then?

TOM / Cut his throat! That's what I'll do! Or find someone to do it for me.

JOHNSON / My God, sir! The strength of your conscience is matched only by the weakness of your purse I see.

Act I Scene II. An Hotel Room

TOM / Are you such an impenetrable blockhead as to believe he will help me with even a single farthing, let alone a pocketful of Scarborough 'small change'?

JOHNSON / Not if you treat him the way you have in the past.

TOM / How should I treat him then?

JOHNSON / Lure him like a trout. Tickle his fancy, caress his pride, stroke his ego. *'Stroke it well, see it swell'*.

TOM / As if it isn't big enough already! I cannot bring myself to speak kindly of the man, let alone flatter him.

JOHNSON / Can you bring yourself to starve?

TOM / Rather than crawl to my brother on bended knee, yes.

JOHNSON / Well I can't.
(*putting hat and coat on*) So, I bid you goodbye, Sir.

TOM / No, Johnson, please stay. You'll be a distraction for me, and besides, I can't do this without you.

JOHNSON / Do nothing you mean? You seem to need little help in achieving that aim… (*pauses for thought*) Though before I leave, perhaps we should take lunch. Things always make more sense on a full stomach, and mine is far from full.

TOM / (*grabbing jacket*) See. I knew there was a reason for my keeping you. Come. My treat.

[EXIT *TOM* WITH A HAPPY AIR. STARING AFTER HIM IN SILENT DISBELIEF A RESIGNED *JOHNSON* THEN FOLLOWS HIM OUT]

ACT I SCENE III. THE HOTEL AFTER A HEARTY MEAL

[*TOM* AND *JOHNSON* ARE RELAXING WITH BRANDY AND CIGARS. *COLONEL CHUMLEY* ENTERS]

TOM / I remember the Scarborough Opera House was the place to be Johnson, used to be a good social gathering - talking of which, look who has just come in. My old friend, Colonel Chumley.
(*standing*) My dear Colonel. I am overjoyed to meet you here.

CHUMLEY / My dear Tom. This is an unexpected pleasure! Are you here in Scarborough for your brother's wedding?

TOM / Wedding?

JOHNSON / (*rising to his feet, offering his hand*) Had you said 'funeral' then we could have said it truly was a 'pleasure'.

CHUMLEY / What? Good, long suffering, Johnson? Still serving with Tom Fro'tham I see.

JOHNSON / Alas yes, sir. I've been 'starving' with him since I saw your lordship last.

TOM / (*mock laughter*) Why, Johnson is an amusing rogue, rather attached to me. There is no ridding myself of him it seems.

JOHNSON / True, sir, as my master says, there is no seducing me away from his service. (*low*) At least till he's able to pay my wages.

TOM / Johnson, I think it's about time our baggage was unpacked. And get the hotel to store that damn chest somewhere, I don't want to be falling over it in the dark.

JOHNSON / Oh yes, sir. The baggage! I trust, sir, I should insist the hotel manager is very particular where he shoves the chest?

TOM / Get along, you rascal!

Act I Scene III. The Hotel After A Hearty Meal

[*JOHNSON* EXITS, LEAVING HIS BRANDY ON THE TABLE]

TOM / Join me in a drink, Colonel.

CHUMLEY / Thank you, I will.

TOM / (*signaling a waiter who isn't there*) Waiter! A large cognac for the Colonel if you please, put it on my bill.

[THEY SIT. THE DRINK NEVER ARRIVES]

TOM / So, my brother's getting married, eh? Tell me, colonel, are you acquainted with my proposed sister-in-law?

CHUMLEY / Only by reputation. She lives with her widowed father, Sir Tobias Coombs, not far from here in a lonely, old, rambling house. She never goes out, nor receives any company.

TOM / Really? Why is that?

CHUMLEY / To prevent any 'misfortunes', her father says. She receives her tuition at home: the parson of the parish gives her piano lessons, the housekeeper gives her singing lessons, her father teaches her dance and her nursemaid dresses and feeds her.

TOM / An odd mixture of schooling. Still I suppose they do things differently in the country.

CHUMLEY / Quite, poor girl, she'll be scared out of her wits on her wedding night, I'm sure she doesn't know a man from a woman but by his beard and his britches. Nobody has free admission there except our old acquaintance, Dame Cummins - and she is not a great example of the differences that separate our genders – but anyway it was she who procured your brother this match.

TOM / Is the girl's wealth considerable?

CHUMLEY / Three thousand a year, and a good sum of money independent of her father as well.

TOM / Curses! Just my usual luck! Why couldn't Dame Cummins have thought of me instead of my brother for such a prize catch?

CHUMLEY / My dear, Tom! I wouldn't swear it is not too late.

TOM / Not too late? I don't follow.

CHUMLEY / Listen, Tom. I know for sure your brother has not yet laid eyes upon the young lady, and, what is more, he has quarreled with his procurer.

TOM / Dame Cummins! - My dear Colonel, what an idea you have given me!

CHUMLEY / Exactly! Pursue it if you can, and I promise my assistance gladly.

TOM / What is your interest in all this, Colonel?

CHUMLEY / Well, besides my natural contempt for his lordship, I have the added complication of a rival love interest between us.

TOM / What? Has my brother been seeing your old flame? Not the young widow, Sophia?

CHUMLEY / Not to put too fine a point on it, Tom, my circumstances are a little complicated at the present time. You see, I came to Scarborough a month ago to meet the lady you mention, but she has gone out of her way since to avoid me.

TOM / Had you done anything to provoke such a reaction?

CHUMLEY / Not knowingly. So to keep myself from boredom, I have been diverting my attentions to the beauty of the wife of our good friend, Lovelace, instead.

TOM / Amanda? I have not met her, but I have heard she is a wonder of rare beauty for her years.

Act I Scene III. The Hotel After A Hearty Meal

CHUMLEY / Yes, Amanda, and she is indeed. Plus, what with Lovelace being careless of the treasure he possesses, and my lodgings being situated in the same house, fate has handed me unbridled opportunity to make my interests known to her. It has certainly diverted my mind from the disappointment of the widow, Sophia, in the last fortnight.

TOM / Women! No doubt she'll soon be resuming her hold over you, especially as the one you seek to amuse yourself with is the wife of your good friend. But my ass of a brother is an admirer of Amanda's as well, is he?

CHUMLEY / Yes, though I believe she most heartily despises him. Why not come with me to my lodgings? You can see her beauty for yourself and meet your old friend, Lovelace.

TOM / I would love to, Colonel, but first I must pay my respects to his lordship. Perhaps you can direct me to his lodgings.

CHUMLEY / Walk with me. I pass by them on the way. He rises late every day, (*checking his pocket watch*) and as it's not quite two o'clock he should still be there.

TOM / (*standing*) Excellent. I'll collect Johnson and meet you at the desk. – (*picking up his brandy*) You didn't drink your brandy, Colonel. (*gestures to Johnson's unfinished drink*)

CHUMLEY / Was that mine? I thought it was Johnson's. Oh well, shame to waste it. (*downs it in one*)

[THEY DOWN THEIR DRINKS AND EXIT]

ACT I SCENE IV. LORD FRONTBOTHAM'S LODGINGS

[***LORD F*** IS ALONE DRESSED IN HIS LONG-JOHN UNDERWEAR]

LORD F / (*spoken to his reflection in a dress mirror in the centre of the room*) Well, well, well, 'tis an unbelievable pleasure to be a man of quality, or strike me dumb! Even the bores of this northern spa have learned the respect due a title. (*calls*) Delaflote!

[***DELAFLOTE***, THE OVERLY DRAMATIC, EFFEMINATE FRENCH VALET OF **LORD F**, MINCES INTO THE ROOM. THEIR BEHAVIOUR TOWARDS EACH OTHER IS MORE AKIN TO LONG SUFFERING HUSBAND AND WIFE THAN MASTER AND SERVANT]

DELAFLOTE / (*thick French accent*) Milord?

LORD F / Have you been to Muddy Moat Hall to announce my intended arrival yet?

DELAFLOTE / *Pas encore*, milord.

LORD F / In English, imbecile!

DELAFLOTE / Not yet, (*under his breath*) *cochon*.

LORD F / Good. You need not go till Saturday now.

[***LORD F*** CONTINUES GAZING AT HIMSELF IN THE MIRROR, THEN SEES THE REFLECTION OF ***DELAFLOTE*** BEHIND HIM, MIMICKING HIS HEAD ANGLES. HE STOPS AND LOOKS AT ***DELAFLOTE*** IN THE REFLECTION. ***DELAFLOTE*** STOPS]

LORD F / (*dismissively*) That will be all.

DELAFLOTE / Oui, milord.

[***DELAFLOTE*** TURNS AND EXITS THE ROOM]

Act I Scene IV. Lord Frontbotham's Lodgings

LORD F / (*to mirror*) I am in no particular haste to view my intended spouse, I shall sacrifice a day or two more in the pursuit of Lovelace's wife. Amanda is a charming creature, and good in the saddle I'll warrant, and strike-me-down-ugly if she doesn't think likewise of me, the great Lord Fro'tham!

[***DELAFLOTE*** RE-ENTERS THE ROOM. ***LORD F*** IS STILL ADMIRING HIMSELF IN THE MIRROR]

DELAFLOTE / Milord…(*pauses on seeing Lord F's ridiculous affair with his reflection*) …If I may interrupt le 'appy couple…

LORD F / What is it now, man?

DELAFLOTE / De 'aberdasher and de seamstress be all ready, if your lordship pleases, with your *habillement*.

LORD F / Good, send them in.

DELAFLOTE / (*calling*) Messieurs! Entrez!

[THE ***TAILOR*** AND THE ***SEAMSTRESS*** ENTER AND PLACE OR HANG THEIR GOODS ON DISPLAY FOR ***LORD F*** THEN STEP BACK EXPECTANTLY]

LORD F / (*still looking in mirror*) So gentlemen, I am hoping you have taken great pains to prove yourselves masters in your professions… (*noticing one is an attractive female*) …and 'mistresses'. A man of such style and quality as I cannot be seen in anything but the finest there is to offer.

TAILOR / I think I may presume, Mr Front-bottom…

DELAFLOTE / (*interrupting, punishing*) Milord, to you! You imbecile! Lord. And it is 'Fro'tham', not… (*takes great delight in saying the next words*) 'Front Bottom'!

TAILOR / My lord (*forced*) 'Fro'tham'?

DELAFLOTE / (*deliberate*) 'Fro'tham'

TAILOR / 'Fro'tham' – I ask your lordship's pardon, my lord. I hope, my lord, that your lordship will be pleased with all I have brought your lordship today. As accomplished a wardrobe as was ever worn by an English nobleman. So with your lordship's permission?

LORD F / Yes, yes, but first let my people arrange the mirrors so I may see myself in front and behind. I like to see myself from all angles.
- Delaflote! My mirrors.

DELAFLOTE / M'lord.

[MIRRORS ARE POSITIONED BY *DELAFLOTE*]

LORD F / Hurry up man, I haven't got all day. The ladies await my pleasure, yes indeed!

[*DELAFLOTE* PAUSES EYEING THE VIEW IN THE MIRROR THEN THE GIRTH OF LORD F]

DELAFLOTE / Perhaps if the mirrors were a little wider, milord.

LORD F / Wider! What on earth do I want with wider mirrors? Get on with it, man!

[*TOM* AND *JOHNSON* ARRIVE AT THE OPEN DOOR AND WATCH UNNOTICED FOR A WHILE]

TOM / (*low to Johnson as they arrive*) I hear the unmistakable tones of an imbecile, Johnson.

DELAFLOTE / Meester Tailor, *s'il vous plaît*. (*impatiently*) Come, come!

[*TAILOR* STEPS FORWARD OFFERING THE DRESS SUIT]

TAILOR / My Lord.

TOM / (*low voice to Johnson*) My gentleman brother must be a favourite at court with so many people at his service.

JOHNSON / (*low voice back to Tom*) No, it's 'courting' these people come to make him a favourite at, sir

Act I Scene IV. Lord Frontbotham's Lodgings

TOM / (*low voice*) Good heavens! To what depths of taste have women fallen that a laced coat should hold the power to decide whether a man is good enough.

JOHNSON / (*low voice*) Tailors and jewellers hold the power to lead many women astray these days, sir.

TOM / (*low voice*) I fear you may be right. Let us observe how the other half lives for a moment.

LORD F / (*to tailor, examining himself in the mirror*) Death and eternal tortures, man! I say the jacket is too wide by a good foot.

TAILOR / My lord. Had it been any tighter it would neither have closed nor buttoned up.

LORD F / Rats to the buttons, sir! Can anything be worse than this? As God is my witness, it hangs on my shoulders like a loose gown.

TAILOR / It is not for me to dispute your lordship's taste.

TOM / (*low to Johnson*) Taste?

JOHNSON / (*low to Tom*) The respect money begets is rarely true, nor without malice in some form, sir.

TOM / (*low to Johnson*) Respect? Damn him for the conceited dandy he is! Time for me to make my entrance.

[***TOM*** STEPS FORWARD INTO THE ROOM]

TOM / (*aloud*) Brother, I am your humble servant, though not perhaps so humble as the multitude of servants I see before you.

LORD F / (*sometimes pronouncing 'o' as 'a'*) My word, 'Tam'! I did not expect you in England.
(*to tailor, taking off jacket*) Look here, tailor, I shall never be happy in this nauseous wrapping gown, pray get me another with all possible haste, this one has my eternal loathing.

[*TAILOR* STEPS AWAY CARRYING THE JACKET, SHAKING HIS HEAD]

LORD F / Well, well, 'Tam', but you haven't told me what brings you to Scarborough. Here to witness my happy occasion?

TOM / Happy occasion? Seeing my elder brother is always a happy occasion.

LORD F / Ha, ha, broke again, eh, 'Tam'? I'm surprised you haven't heard my news. It's the talk of the 'tawn'. One must always have something for a 'tawn' to talk about, or the ladies would be disappointed.

TOM / I have no doubt you give the ladies plenty to talk about.

LORD F / How I have left them all broken hearted? I can understand their wretchedness.
(*to seamstress*) Seamstress? Are you not seeing to me?

SEAM / Right away, my lord Fron... Fro'tham. Here –

[SHE HOLDS A DRESS SHIRT IN EACH HAND]

SEAM / Does your lordship see anything which takes his fancy?

LORD F / (*looking her up and* down) Indeed I do.

SEAM / May I suggest this one, your lordship, for so noble a body?

[SHE PASSES A DRESS SHIRT WHICH HE TRIES ON]

SEAM / (*coy*) I hope your lordship is pleased with my ruffles.

LORD F / I love them, indeed I do! (*squeezing her behind*)

Act I Scene IV. Lord Frontbotham's Lodgings

SEAM / (*jumps & giggles, pleased*) Oh!

LORD F / Bring my bill tomorrow, you little minx, I'll show you a lord of the realm is not backward in giving a lady a little extra for her 'personal' attention.

SEAM / (*enticingly*) Oh yes, your lordship. I shall bring it tomorrow, personally.

[***SEAMSTRESS*** STEPS AWAY BEAMING SMUGLY AT THE ***TAILOR*** WHO PASSES NEXT ITEM TO ***LORD F***]

TAILOR / (*offering*) Stockings, my lord.

LORD F / (*trying on knee high dress stockings*) Mr Tailor, a word with you. The calves of these stockings are thickened a little too much, they make my legs look like a porter's.

TAILOR / My lord, I think they look very well.

LORD F / But you are not so good a judge on these things as I am. I have studied them all my life. Therefore pray let the next pair be the thickness of a crown piece less.

TAILOR / Indeed, my lord, they are the same kind I had the honour of fitting his Highness with in town last Michaelmas.

LORD F / Very possibly, Mr Tailor, but that was making allowances for the fatigues of Winter. You should always remember that if you make a nobleman's Spring legs as robust as his Autumnal calves, you commit a monstrous impropriety. Now pass me some shoes.

[***TAILOR*** PASSES SHOES, ***LORD F*** KEEPS THE SOCKS ON]

LORD F / (*putting on shoes*) Listen, now, these shoes look all right but they don't fit me.

TAILOR / My lord, I think they fit you very well.

LORD F / They hurt me just below the instep.

TAILOR / Let me feel.
(*feeling the feet*) No, my lord, they don't hurt you there.

LORD F / Are you telling me I have no feelings?

TAILOR / Your lordship may feel whatever he thinks fit, but the shoe doesn't hurt you. I think I understand my trade.

LORD F / (*taking off shoes*) By all that's good and powerful, you are an incomprehensible, conceited fool! Your shoes may look good, but they don't fit a proper sized foot.

TAILOR / (*taking shoes*) My lord, I have worked for half the people of quality in this town for the last twenty years, I assure you I know when a shoe fits.

LORD F / Well, be gone about your business of crippling half the town with your instruments of 'tarture' then, I will suffer with my old shoes.

[***TAILOR*** STEPS AWAY WITH THEM SHAKING HIS HEAD]

TAILOR / I assure you, sir, they are a perfect fit, (*mutters to seamstress*) for his fat feet.

LORD F / (*taking off the socks*) What was that?

TAILOR / Only that they are a fine fit, your lordship.

LORD F / As you say.
(*calls*) My kerchief?

[THE ***TAILOR*** AND THE ***SEAMSTRESS*** STEP FORWARD EACH HOLDING KERCHIEFS]

LORD F / (*to Tailor*) Confound it man, what monstrosity is this? I want to attract the ladies, not scare them off!
(*he takes one from the seamstress*) Now, this is more in keeping with the times. (*sniffing it*) Such delightful perfume!

Act I Scene IV. Lord Frontbotham's Lodgings

SEAM / Thank you, my lordship, I carried it tucked in my blouse for safe keeping.

LORD F / He, he, bring me two more tomorrow, freshly perfumed. -Right. You can both go now, and Mr Tailor, next time I expect you to bring me something more fitting for the current season.

[*LORD F* DISMISSES THEM WITH A WAVE OF HIS HAND]

[THEY GATHER UP GOODS AND USHERED IMPATIENTLY BY *DELAFLOTE* THEY EXIT, THE *TAILOR* UNHAPPILY, THE *SEAMSTRESS* WITH A SMUG GRIN]

LORD F / (*dressing*) There, now the business of the morning is pretty well over. It just remains for me to finish my grooming.

[*DELAFLOTE* SITS DOWN AS IF HIS WORK IS FINISHED]

LORD F / Get up, man! Stir that featherbrained, gallic head of yours and see to it my carriage is ready.

DELAFLOTE / (*exiting with his nose in the air and a dismissive flick of his hand*) Pah!

TOM / Now your people of business are gone, brother, I hope I may gain a quarter of an hour's audience with you.

LORD F / Goodness, 'Tam', I must beg you'll excuse me at this time. I have a prior engagement which I could not break even 'far' the salvation of mankind.
(*Calling out*) Delaflote! Is my carriage at the door?

DELAFLOTE / (*off, sarcastic*) It is ready for your 'lordship's every desire'. (*quieter, but audible to all*) Pig face.

LORD F / What was that?

[*DELAFLOTE* RE-ENTERS WITH HAT, GLOVES AND CANE FOR *LORD F*]

DELAFLOTE / (*entering*) *Vitesse! Vitesse!* And the coachman asks you sit on the right side today.

LORD F / The right side? He wishes to deprive the flower sellers on the parade their daily pleasure of my finery as I drive past?

DELAFLOTE / *Non*, he said he wishes to bring *équilibre* back to the carriage.

LORD F / Equilibre? I'm sure the carriage driver never used such a word in his entire life.

DELAFLOTE / *Non*, he said, "The ruddy carriage has developed a list" but I did not wish to offend such regal ears as yours by repeating it, milord. *(turning to leave)*

LORD F / And what else did he say which you cannot repeat?

DELAFLOTE / *(exiting)* I could not possibly repeat it, milord.

[***DELAFLOTE* EXITS**]

LORD F / Damned staff. I don't get such impertinence in London. I shall be glad when I return there, - five thousand pounds the richer.
(putting on his hat and gloves) You will excuse me I hope, brother.

TOM / Will you be back for dinner?

LORD F / As God is my judge, I cannot say. I may dine with friends at The Regency.

TOM / Shall I meet you there? I must talk with you.

LORD F / That I'm afraid may not be proper, for those I normally eat with are people of good conversation, and you know, 'Tam', your education has been a little *lacking*.
But there are commoners in town, very good beef-eating ordinary people – I assume you can eat beef, 'Tam'?

[A DISTANT CLOCK STRIKES TWO]

Act I Scene IV. Lord Frontbotham's Lodgings

LORD F / My word, is that the time?
(*hurrying to the door*) However, my dear brother, I am glad to see you in England, that I am.

TOM / But when....

[*LORD F* EXITS]

TOM / Hell and furies! Do I have to put up with this?

JOHNSON / Honestly, sir, I could give him a knock about the head myself!

TOM / Justifiably so, Johnson. For my part though, I'll stem my anger by plotting my revenge. Come, Johnson, lay your thick head against mine and in calm cold blood, let us plot his downfall together.

JOHNSON / Oh don't you worry yourself about that, sir. I have plotted it a thousand times before - with a hot poker.

[FRONT DOOR BELL RINGS, OFF]

TOM / Tempting as your option sounds I think we should settle for a more subtle approach first, Johnson.

DELAFLOTE / (*off*) Bonjour, madam.

CUMMINS / (*off, angry*) Where is his Lordship?

TOM / (*to Johnson, cocking his ear*) Listen.

DELAFLOTE / (*off, curt*) Out. Goodbye.

CUMMINS / (*off, angry*) Out! Is that all? Don't they teach you elementary manners back in your heathen country.

DELAFLOTE / (*off*) No, madam, they teach us English manners.

CUMMINS / (*off*) Your ignorance is truly astonishing. I suppose they heard your grating Gallic accent and supposed you could cook. - When will he be back?

TOM / *(to Johnson)* Dame Cummins!

DELAFLOTE / *(off)* I cannot say, madam.

CUMMINS / *(off, in anger)* Out whoring I've no doubt! And I suppose he's left no money for me has he? I am to be well rewarded for my services indeed! Truly, my suspicions were well founded.

JOHNSON / *(listening)* A dissatisfied Dame Cummins.

[THE VOICES APPROACH]

DELAFLOTE / *(off)* His lordship left no instructions to hand you any monies, madam.

[**DAME CUMMINS** ENTERS THE ROOM STILL TALKING TO **DELAFLOTE** AND NOT NOTICING THE TWO MEN WAITING THERE]

CUMMINS / So! He refuses to advance me a petty sum when I am about to make him master of a fine ship! Let him see the consequences, the ungrateful…

TOM / *(unseen by Cummins)* Afternoon, my dear lady.

[**DELAFLOTE** TAKES THIS OPPORTUNITY TO MAKE GOOD HIS ESCAPE]

CUMMINS / *(Wheeling around and seeing Tom)* Ha! Strippling! What are you doing here? Have you spent it all, eh? Come to touch his lordship for assistance?

TOM / I'd rather cut his lordship's throat than touch him.

CUMMINS / My God, sir! -But thinking about it, I could help you do almost as much harm, and without fear of getting your hands burnt for it.

TOM / How so? Do tell, old Mrs Mischief, I'm all ears.

CUMMINS / Why, you must have heard, I have done you the kindness of finding a bride for your brother.

Act I Scene IV. Lord Frontbotham's Lodgings

TOM / (*sarcastic*) And for that 'I' am very much in your debt, madam.

CUMMINS / You could be more so by the wedding day, young man, so you mind your tone with me. -The lady is heiress to a great fortune.

TOM / So I understand.

CUMMINS / Now, you must know, young strippling, your brother is a rogue.

TOM / Indeed.

CUMMINS / He has given me a pledge of one thousand pounds for helping him obtain this fortune, and has promised me as much again, in cash, upon the day of the marriage.

TOM / The sly old fox. So that's how he did it.

CUMMINS / But I understand, from a friend, he never plans to pay me.

TOM / Sounds familiar.

CUMMINS / However, if you were to be a generous young rogue and secure me five thousand pounds for my services, then I would help YOU to the lady instead.

TOM / Better and better! But how the devil could you do that?

CUMMINS / Not with the devil's aid, I assure you. But first, shut the door. I don't trust that French halfwit, his ears stick out too far, he hears everything he shouldn't I'll warrant. And he puts his mouth about in a way more befitting of a woman, so I am led to believe from my housekeeper.

[THEY CLOSE THE DOOR]

CUMMINS / (*lowered voice*) That's better. Now, my plan. You see, your brother's face has not been seen by a single soul of the intended's family.

TOM / How absurd. Still, I can see why you kept him apart till now, a thousand pounds is a lot of money to lose.

CUMMINS / No, 'twas more, doubly so. But anyway, the whole business has been handled by me and all the letters go through my hands. Sir Tobias Coombs, that's the father of the young girl, is peeved at your brother's decision to delay the wedding a few days in order to *'recover from the fatigues of his journey'*.

TOM / My brother was never anything but a fool. And a vain, arrogant fool at that.

CUMMINS / That's the truth. But now you can go to Muddy Moat Hall in his place. I'll give you a letter of introduction, and if you don't marry the girl before sunset tomorrow, you deserve to be hanged by sunrise.

TOM / Agreed! Agreed! But, as for your reward…

CUMMINS / I'll wager you have not even small change to your name, no, further, not even a farthing in your pocket, I can see it in your face.

TOM / Not a cent, by Jupiter! Am I that easy to read?

CUMMINS / (*sighing*) Must I advance you then? Very well, be at my lodgings this evening and I'll see what can be done, we'll sign and seal the deal then. Now I must be gone, arrangements have to be put in place. Remember, this evening, six o'clock, don't be late.

TOM / You can rely on me, madam.

[***DAME CUMMINS*** EXITS, HER VOICE IS HEARD ADMONISHING ***DELAFLOTE***]

CUMMINS / (*off*) Out of my way, gallic hound. And don't shrug your shoulders in that way at me!

DELAFLOTE / (*off*) Pah!

Act I Scene IV. Lord Frontbotham's Lodgings

[A DOOR SLAMS WITHIN]

TOM / So, Johnson, fortune at last takes care of just causes! We are well on our way to riches.

JOHNSON / Aye, sir, if the devil doesn't step between the cup and the lip as he has in the past.

TOM / That's the truth, and I'm almost afraid he's working against us now.

JOHNSON / Already?

TOM / Johnson, you know I have played many a roguish trick in the past in order for us to eat, but this is a cheat of such grand scale, I find myself increasingly at odds with my conscience.

JOHNSON / Then I suggest you make out your will at once, sir.

TOM / No, my conscience will not force me to starve, but I will give heed to it. I will try appealing to my brother one last time. Let him decide the direction the wheel of fate points.

END OF ACT I

ACT II

ACT II SCENE I. LOVELACE'S LODGINGS. THE DRAWING ROOM

[*MR LOVELACE* AND HIS LOVELY WIFE *AMANDA* ARE TALKING OVER CUPS OF TEA]

LOVELACE / How do you like the lodgings, Amanda? For my part, I am so pleased with them I shall hardly leave them while we stay here, as long as you are happy.

AMANDA / As your wife, I am pleased with everything which pleases you, my dearest, otherwise I would not come to Scarborough at all, though I think we can hardly afford them.

LOVELACE / Well, perhaps a little of the tedium of this sleepy seaside resort will sweeten the pleasures of our town retreat when we return to it. I have a couple of business interests I hope to bring to fruition when we return.

AMANDA / That pleasing prospect will be my main source of inspiration whilst I am here, enduring those empty pleasures it is so fashionable to be fond of these days.

LOVELACE / Yes, and I am guilty of most of them, I admit, and they are indeed empty, yet there are delights to divert an honest man's attentions which are harmless enough entertainment for a virtuous woman too, and not too heavy on the purse. Good music is one, and truly I feel - making a small allowance for taste - the theatre might be considered another.

AMANDA / A good play, I must confess, does have some small charm. What did you think of the one you saw last night?

LOVELACE / To be honest, I did not pay much attention, my mind was for some time drawn to admire the workmanship of nature.

AMANDA / Workmanship of nature?

Act II Scene I. Lovelace's Lodgings

LOVELACE / Yes, in the face of a woman sat some distance from me, she was so exquisitely handsome.

AMANDA / So exquisitely handsome?

LOVELACE / Why do you repeat my words, my dear?

AMANDA / You seemed to speak them with such pleasure, I thought I might oblige you with their echo.

LOVELACE / There is no need for alarm, dearest. I viewed her as one would a fine work of art; with admiration, not with love.

AMANDA / Take heed trusting in such fine distinctions. But, tell me, was it only your eyes that wished to know her better?

LOVELACE / I assure you, my love, the only stirrings I have are solely for you.

AMANDA / But had I been in your place, my tongue, I fancy, would have been curious too.

LOVELACE / Tongue? How so, my love?

AMANDA / I would have asked her name. You have a tongue in your head, as your wife I know you are quite capable of using it, so pray tell me, who was she?

LOVELACE / Indeed I cannot.

AMANDA / You cannot tell me, your wife?

LOVELACE / Upon my honour, I did not ask. But why so interested, my love?

AMANDA / I thought I had just cause to be.

LOVELACE / You thought wrongly, Amanda. Turn it around and let it be your story. If you came home and told me you had seen a handsome man, should I be jealous because you have eyes?

AMANDA / If I told you he was exquisitely so, and that I gazed upon him in admiration, would you not think it possible I might go one step further?

LOVELACE / Further?

AMANDA / And enquire after his name?

LOVELACE / Hmm. Then you say there is no difference, Amanda, between the language of my sex and yours?

AMANDA / Difference?

LOVELACE / Yes, difference. Women often say things by halves, while men, on the other hand, may be guilty of a little exaggeration here and there. Even though we may both be thinking the same thoughts, Amanda, we may differ in our wording of them.

[DOORBELL RINGS IN DISTANCE]

LOVELACE / (*in relief*) Saved by the bell.
-Were you expecting visitors, my sweet?

AMANDA / Who could I possibly be expecting here in Scarborough? Handsome or otherwise.

[**WITHERS** THE BUTLER ENTERS]

WITHERS / Madam, there is a lady at the door who wishes to know whether your ladyship is receiving company.

AMANDA / For me?

WITHERS / (*offering a card on a tray*) Her card.

AMANDA / (*reading card*) Oh dear!

LOVELACE / What is it, my love?

AMANDA / A relation I have not seen since she was a child. I feel horribly guilty at my lack of attention.
(*to Withers*) Have her walk in, at once, Withers.

Act II Scene I. Lovelace's Lodgings

[*WITHERS* EXITS]

AMANDA / Here's another beauty for you, or at least so I am told, one who has grown to be extremely '*handsome*'.

LOVELACE / Don't be jealous then, if I gaze upon her too.

[ENTER *SOPHIA*]

AMANDA / Sophia! My dear!

SOPHIA / Amanda!

[THE LADIES EMBRACE]

LOVELACE / (*low, to self*) By heavens! It's the same woman!

AMANDA / My, you have grown! It has been so long, how can you ever forgive me.

SOPHIA / Dear Amanda, you haven't changed a bit. I was not expecting to meet you in Scarborough!

AMANDA / Sweet Sophia, I am overjoyed to see you. This is my husband, Mr Lovelace.

LOVELACE / (*takes her hand, kisses it, and continues to hold it*) Charmed, madam. My wife has deprived me of your beauty all these years.

AMANDA / Sophia is my cousin, dearest. One I hope you will soon be better acquainted with.

[A DOORBELL RINGS IN THE DISTANCE]

LOVELACE / Cousin?

AMANDA / My late Uncle Eustace, ma-ma's late brother, married late in life, lateness being the only thing he truly excelled at.

LOVELACE / (*still holding Sophia's hand and gazing at her*) I am grateful for his tardiness. Your mother must have been a strikingly beautiful woman.

[*SOPHIA* LOOKS DOWN AT HER HAND, *LOVELACE* LOOKS DOWN THEN UP AT *AMANDA* WHO LOOKS AT HIM THEN DOWN AT *SOPHIA*'S HAND STILL IN HIS HAND WHICH HE QUICKLY DROPS IN REALISATION]

SOPHIA / How sweet.

AMANDA / How did you know I would be staying in Scarborough, Sophia?

SOPHIA / Colonel Chumley told me you were staying here. In fact he could talk of little else when I saw him last.

AMANDA / Ah yes, the good Colonel lodges here as well. He didn't mention he knew you.

[RE-ENTER *WITHERS*]

WITHERS / Sir, my Lord Fro'tham presents his humble service to you. He asks, if convenient with yourself, that he may pay you a visit.

LOVELACE / Give my compliments to his lordship. I shall be glad to see him.

[*WITHERS* EXITS]

LOVELACE / If you are not acquainted with his lordship, Sophia, I am sure you will be entertained by his character.

AMANDA / Though I am more moved to pity than humour for a man nature has chosen not to be born an idiot, yet who works so hard trying to pass as one.

SOPHIA / If he is as you describe then I am eager to see him for myself.

[ENTER *LORD F*]

LORD F / Dear Lovelace, I am your most humble servant.

LOVELACE / My lord, I am yours. You know my wife.

LORD F / Madam, I am your ladyship's obedient slave.

Act II Scene I. Lovelace's Lodgings

LOVELACE / And this lady, my lord, is Sophia, a relation of my wife's.

LORD F / (*bowing*) The most beautiful race of people upon this earth - strike me down! Madam, my card.

[***LORD F*** HANDS ***SOPHIA*** HIS CARD]

SOPHIA / I am honoured, Lord...? (*looking at card, trying to work out the pronunciation*)

LORD F / (*interrupting*) ...Fro'tham, madam. Lord Fro'tham.

SOPHIA / (*surprised*) Oh.

LORD F / My dear Lovelace, I am overjoyed you consider continuing to stay in Scarborough, that I am, strap my vitals! but for 'Gad's' sake, how has your good wife been able to endure the fatigue of country life for so long?

AMANDA / My life here has been far from that, my lord, it has been a very quiet one.

LORD F / Why, that's the fatigue I speak of, madam. For it is impossible to be quiet without thinking, and thinking to me is the greatest fatigue in the world.

AMANDA / Does your lordship not love reading, then?

LORD F / Oh, passionately, madam, but I never think about what I read.

AMANDA / Pity the poor writers. How do you occupy your mind then?

LORD F / Well, I rise in the morning, madam, at twelve o'clock - I am quite the human sundial, you know. I don't rise sooner because it is the worst thing in the world for the complexion, not that I pretend to be an Adonis mind, but a man must endeavour to look decent lest he makes so unpleasant a sight in the Royal box that the ladies would be compelled to avert their eyes to watch the play.

AMANDA / (*subtle, mocking agreement*) Heaven forbid!

LORD F / Quite. So at twelve o'clock, as I said, I rise. Now, if I find it a good day, I 'resalve' to take the exercise of riding. I always find a good ride in the morning gives one a good appetite for the rest of the day, don't you agree? Then upon my return I change and, after dinner, relax, perhaps at a concert.

SOPHIA / Oh, so your lordship is fond of music?

LORD F / Oh, passionately, Sophia, on Tuesdays and Saturdays. For that is when there is always the best company, so one is not expected to undergo the fatigue of listening.

AMANDA / And what are your lordship's thoughts on the opera?

LORD F / I adore it, madam. There is Lady Tattle, Lady Prattle, Lady Titter, Lady Sneer, Lady Giggle and Lady Grin, as I have named them – not to their face mind. They all have their boxes in the front and whilst a favourite aria is being sung are the prettiest company in the 'warld' - strap my vitals! May we hope for the honour of seeing you added to our society, madam?

AMANDA / Alas, my lord, I am the worst company in the world at such an event. I am so inclined to listen to the music.

LORD F / Why, madam, that is very pardonable in church, but a monstrous inattention in polite society.

SOPHIA / Isn't your lordship sometimes obliged to attend the weighty affairs of the nation?

LORD F / Madam, as to weighty affairs, I leave them to weighty heads. I never intend mine to be a burden to my body.

SOPHIA / Really, my lord? But you are a pillar of the state.

LORD F / An ornamental pillar, madam, ornamental. Should I ever partake in any such fatigues, then - rat me! - the whole building would crumble to the ground!

Act II Scene I. Lovelace's Lodgings

AMANDA / Surely a fine gentleman such as yourself spends a great deal of time taking care of his affairs. You have given us no account of them as yet.

LORD F / (*mistaking the meaning of 'affairs'*)
So! You are interested in my *affairs*, eh?
- Oh Lord, madam. I had forgotten - I have something to tell your ladyship in strictest confidence. Mr Lovelace, you need not be so jealous as to listen to what I say.

LOVELACE / Not I, my lord, I am too fashionably modern a husband to pry into the secrets of my wife.
Come, Sophia - such a pretty name - let us get better acquainted and leave them to their secrets.

[EXIT **LOVELACE** AND **SOPHIA**]

LORD F / Now we are alone, there is something I have to tell you.

AMANDA / Whatever is so important that it cannot be shared?

LORD F / I am desperately in love with you, or strike me speechless!

[**LORD F** SQUEEZES HER BEHIND MAKING WHAT HE, AND ONLY HE, THINKS IS AN AMOROUS SOUND, THEN LEANS IN TO KISS HER.
AMANDA RETALIATES IN SHOCK AND SURPRISE, AND STRIKES HIM ABOUT THE HEAD]

AMANDA / (*striking him*) How dare you lay your hands upon my person!

LORD F / Ow!

AMANDA / That, sir, returns your passion, you impudent fool!

LORD F / Good God, madam, I am a peer of the realm!

[**LOVELACE** RUSHES BACK IN]

LOVELACE / What the devil is going on? Did you accost my wife, sir? Answer me now!

LORD F / She boxed me about my ears!

AMANDA / He tried to make love to me, in front of my own husband!

LOVELACE / Is this true, sir! Then my wife's honour is at stake. There is only one way to settle this - if you be a man! Catch!

[*LOVELACE* DRAWS SWORDS FROM A DISPLAY STAND, THROWS ONE TO *LORD F*, WHICH CLATTERS UNCAUGHT ON THE FLOOR AT *LORD F*'S FEET.
HE HOLDS THE OTHER AGAINST *LORD F*'S CHEST]

AMANDA / What have I started? Someone part them for Heaven's sake!

LOVELACE / Damn it man! Pick up your sword!

[*LORD F* LEANS FORWARD DELIBERATELY ONTO *LOVELACE'S* SWORD TIP - BUT NOT SO IT PENETRATES DEEPLY. HE FALLS DRAMATICALLY TO THE FLOOR]

[THE LADIES SCREAM]

LORD F / Ah! Right through my body, Strap my vitals!

[*WITHERS* RUSHES IN AT THE NOISE]

WITHERS / Whatever's the matter?

LOVELACE / I hope I haven't killed the fool. Though he fell on the blade by his own accord.
(*to Withers*) Call a surgeon quickly.

[*WITHERS* RUSHES OFF]

LORD F / Aye, with all haste, man.

LOVELACE / You have only yourself to blame for this injury.

LORD F / My heart, my bleeding heart. Run through. This is the end. What will the ladies do without me?

LOVELACE / Breathe a sigh of relief, I should imagine.

AMANDA / (*still shocked*) Is he going to die?

[RE-ENTER *WITHERS* HASTILY WITH *DR SALOMON*]

Act II Scene I. Lovelace's Lodgings

WITHERS / (*breathless*) Here's Dr. Salomon, sir. He was just passing the door, rather fortunately.

LOVELACE / Yes indeed. Though if I were a surgeon I'd probably follow the fool around.

LORD F / The most welcome man alive. Over here man.

SALOMON / Stand back, stand back. Stand back, please gentlemen, stand back. Lord have mercy on us, did you never see a man run through the body before? Please, stand back.

LORD F / Ugh, Dr. Salomon, I'm a dead man.

SALOMON / A dead man with me here! I laugh at the thought of it, by God.

LOVELACE / Please don't stand prattling, tend to his wounds, sir.

SALOMON / And what if I didn't tend to his wounds at this hour, sir?

LOVELACE / (*exasperated*) Why, then he'll bleed to death, obviously, SIR!

SALOMON / Then I'll fetch him back to life, sir, and get greater reward by his cure. Now, if you are satisfied, let me at him.

[***DR SALOMON*** VIEWS THE WOUND]

SALOMON / Oons! What a gash he has here! Why, sir, a man could drive a coach and six horses into your body.

LORD F / Ohhh!

SALOMON / What the devil did you run this gentleman through with? A scythe?

LOVELACE / A scythe? Let me see his wound.

SALOMON / (*quickly closing the clothing over the wound*) Then you shall dress it, sir, for if anyone else examines it, then I shan't.

LOVELACE / Why, you are the most conceited man I ever saw!

SALOMON / Sir, I am not master of my trade for nothing.

LORD F / Surgeon!

SALOMON / Sir?

LORD F / Is there any hope?

SALOMON / Hope, I cannot tell. What are you willing to give me for a cure?

LORD F / Five hundred 'paunds' with pleasure.

SALOMON / Why, then perhaps there may be hope, but we must avoid further delay. Here, help this gentleman up and carry him to my surgery – that's the best place for him.

LOVELACE / Yes, to squeeze his money from him for such a little scratch.

SALOMON / (*offended*) I beg your pardon?

LOVELACE / I suggest you get him there now, before he changes his mind.

SALOMON / Quickly, man. Help him up.

[**WITHERS** HELPS **LORD F** UP]

LORD F / Dear Lovelace, adieu. If I die, I forgive you, and if I live I hope you will do the same by me.

LOVELACE / I hardly think it worth pursuing any further, so you may be at rest, sir.

LORD F / You are a noble fellow, Lovelace, I shall gain by your example (*lower*) and not marry a frigid wife, slap my vitals!

SALOMON / So carry him off! Carry him off! We will have him in a fever at this rate.

[**WITHERS** HELPS **LORD F** OUT. **DR SALOMON** FOLLOWS]

[ENTER **COLONEL CHUMLEY**]

Act II Scene I. Lovelace's Lodgings

CHUMLEY / I am glad to find you all alive. I saw a wounded peer being led away. For heaven's sake what happened?

LOVELACE / Oh, hello Colonel, just a mere trifle. He made love to my wife in front of my face, so she boxed his ears and I ran him through with a sword, apart from that all's well.

CHUMLEY / Fair game all round then. Whatever drove him to it?

LOVELACE / He seems to thinks his title a passport to every woman's heart below the title of peeress.

CHUMLEY / He's conceited enough to think anything is possible, I hope there is no danger to his life?

LOVELACE / None at all. He's fallen into the hands of a rogue surgeon who I perceive plans to frighten a little money out of him. I saw his wound – it's nothing. He may go to the ball this evening if he so pleases.

CHUMLEY / I am glad you have corrected him without serious injury, or you might have deprived me of a plot I have been contriving with an old acquaintance of yours.

LOVELACE / A plot?

CHUMLEY / His brother, Tom, has arrived and we have plans to save his lordship the trouble of his intended wedding, but we would like your assistance in the matter. So, if these ladies can spare you?

LOVELACE / I'll go with all my heart.

CHUMLEY / Then I shall fetch my coat .
(*turns to Sophie, nods curtly*) Madam Sophia. So good to see you again.

SOPHIA / (*curt sarcasm by return*) Colonel. So good of you to stay so long.

[EXIT **COLONEL CHUMLEY**]

LOVELACE / (*calling*) I'll meet you at the door, Colonel.
(*low, as he retrieves his coat and puts it on, gazing at Sophia as he does*) Though I would wish to stay and gaze a little longer upon this beauty. Good God, how engaging she is!

AMANDA / (*not accusingly*) Husband?

LOVELACE / (*guiltily, thinking he has been caught gazing upon Sophia*) Amanda?

AMANDA / Please, one word with you before you go.

LOVELACE / What is it, my dear?

AMANDA / (*Taking Lovelace aside*) Only a woman's foolish question. What do you think of my cousin here?

LOVELACE / (*in confidence*) Jealous already, Amanda?

AMANDA / (*in confidence*) Not at all. I ask for another reason.

LOVELACE / (*in confidence, guarded*) Why, I confess she is beautiful, but not wishing to slight your relation, she could not satisfy a man in every way as you do, my darling.

AMANDA / I am satisfied.

LOVELACE / Then tell me why you asked?

AMANDA / Tonight I will. Adieu!

LOVELACE / Very well. (*kisses her*)
-Adieu, Sophia. (*kisses Sophia's hand. Then starts to leave, pauses at the door*) Can we expect the pleasure of your company again? At the theatre perhaps?

SOPHIA / Amanda and I have a lot of catching up to do. I'm sure we'll meet again.

LOVELACE / I look forward to it eagerly... (*sees Amanda looking at him*) ...yes, right. *Au revoir*, ladies.

Act II Scene I. Lovelace's Lodgings

[*LOVELACE* EXITS]

AMANDA / My dearest, Sophia.

SOPHIA / Amanda?

AMANDA / Now that we are rid of the men, tell me what it would take to persuade you to come and stay with me, a companion would make the stay here so much more bearable.

SOPHIA / Stay with you? Why, there is only one way in the world you could persuade me.

AMANDA / Oh, tell me. I would give anything to have you here with me.

SOPHIA / By assuring me I would be most welcome.

AMANDA / Why, if that is all it takes you can stay here even tonight.

SOPHIA / Tonight? Why, the people where I lodge would think me quite mad.

AMANDA / Let them think what they like, Sophia.

SOPHIA / If you say so, Amanda, then they shall think what they like. I am a young widow, and I care not what anybody thinks. - Ah, Amanda, it is such a delicious thing to be a young widow!

AMANDA / You'll not convince me that is so.

SOPHIA / Poh! That is because you are in love with your husband. One of life's great follies is to marry the person you love. Marry one you hate. Start as you mean to go on.

AMANDA / But how can you endure being married to one you hate?

SOPHIA / Trust me in this matter, Amanda, wealth makes up for all other shortcomings in a man. Is your husband wealthy, Amanda?

AMANDA / Things have been a little hard of late. – But we have high hopes for the future.

SOPHIA / I suspected as much, it is always the way when women let their hearts rule their heads.

AMANDA / But if a woman loves a man what else can she do?

SOPHIA / If you want to keep the love alive, Amanda, sleep with him, but never marry him. A man's passion always ends with the last bite of the wedding cake.

AMANDA / Did you not sleep with your husband?

SOPHIA / We were like man and wife apart: dull company at the table, even worse in bed. We never agreed on anything except lying apart – twenty miles apart. His bed in the country, mine in a convenient townhouse overlooking the square.

AMANDA / Sophia, forgive me, it is from my world of innocence that I enquire, but I was wondering, if women of good reputation - like ourselves of course - attract the attentions of men other than the type like that buffoon earlier?

SOPHIA / Oh yes, Amanda. There is a particular type of man who makes dreadful mischief amongst this type of women.

AMANDA / Flighty men?

SOPHIA / Oh no, men who keep their brains in their heads and only the one mistress in their bed. Flighty men keep their brains firmly fixed in the southern hemisphere, and are so in love with themselves they have none left for anyone else.

AMANDA / So, one is decent and one is an ass.

SOPHIA / Quite, the only thing the two have in common is their ability to walk upon two legs, though there are times from my experience when they even find this a problem.

AMANDA / If this is their characters, I fancy we have here, even now, one of each.

SOPHIA / One of each?

Act II Scene I. Lovelace's Lodgings

AMANDA / His lordship and Colonel Chumley.

SOPHIA / What wonderful serendipity, Amanda. While the lord, of course, is conspicuously an ass by his own demonstrations today, only yesterday, while taking afternoon tea in the pavilion tea rooms, I had occasion to say there is not a man in town more decent with the ladies than the Colonel. (*throws nose in air*) At least, those worth taking an interest in.

AMANDA / That was the opinion I always used to have of him too.

SOPHIA / (*taken aback*) Used to?

AMANDA / (*taking Sophia's hand*) Sophia, I must let you into a secret. It is not only that fool of a lord who has talked to me of love. Chumley has been interfering too.

SOPHIA / (*parting their hands*) Colonel Chumley? Impossible my dear!

AMANDA / Indeed it is true, though his efforts have been in vain of course. My love for my husband is too dear.

SOPHIA / And nothing could lessen your love for your husband?

AMANDA / Nothing, I am sure.

SOPHIA / Not even if you found he loved another woman?

AMANDA / (*indignant*) Really!

SOPHIA / Really. Why, the way I see it, Amanda, if I ran the risk of having a man called a husband, I would have to accept the danger of being a woman known as a slighted wife.
Did your husband not run off in a mad, wild fit once? Mind you, they all do eventually.

AMANDA / Well, yes, but that was quite a while ago.

SOPHIA / And while he was away you kept your virtue intact?

AMANDA / But of course!

SOPHIA / And if he were to disappear again would you still keep your bed vacant in the hope of his return?

AMANDA / Of all forms of revenge, wronging his bed is... is...

SOPHIA / Is the sweetest, ha, ha! Do I sound foolish?

AMANDA / Quite foolish, though you are, perhaps, more experienced than I in such matters.

SOPHIA / Yet I am still quite innocent.

AMANDA / That I believe you are, but are you saying you will never re-marry?

SOPHIA / Never! You see, being a widow has some rather appealing advantages.

AMANDA / Sophia, you tease me. What possible advantages could there be?

SOPHIA / Well, as a widow, Amanda, the marital bed no longer holds any secrets for me, and nor do I need to save myself for marriage - as I have nothing left to save. So I am free to enjoy any man of my choosing, - or any woman for that matter.

AMANDA / (*embarrassed*) Really, Sophia, the things you say sometimes. I suppose I truly am still so innocent to the ways of the world.

SOPHIA / Truly, I believe you are, Amanda, but my point is; as I have no one to answer to, I can enjoy whatever delights come my way, without the worry and strife normally associated with such endeavours.

AMANDA / Can being so wicked really compensate for the loss of one so dearly loved?

SOPHIA / Loved? Goodness me, my dear Amanda, you are such an old fashioned, romantic fool - but heavens above! I have business at home and I'm half an hour late already.

Act II Scene I. Lovelace's Lodgings

AMANDA / My dear Sophia, as you are to return here with me, I'll give the staff their orders, and walk with you. We have so much to discuss.

SOPHIA / As you say, Amanda, we'll finish our talk as we go.

AMANDA / (*hurrying to the door*) Two shakes of a lamb's tail...

[*AMANDA* EXITS EXCITEDLY]

SOPHIA / (*to self, alone, scheming*) This is a lucky discovery. Lowlife Chumley. False to me and treacherous to his friend by flirting with - of all the women to chose - my innocent, demure cousin. Still, her husband, if I have any skill in judging appearances, would be as happy in my arms as Colonel Chumley would hope to be in hers.
I think I'll make some play and see what comes of it. The woman who can forgive being robbed of a favourite lover must either be a fool or have a devilishly devious plan with which to exact her revenge.

[*AMANDA* RE-ENTERS WEARING HER COAT]

AMANDA / I'm ready, Sophia.

SOPHIA / Are you, Amanda? I wonder.

AMANDA / I've never felt so ready in my life. I have so much to learn.

SOPHIA / More than you could ever imagine. Come on.

[THEY EXIT]

END OF ACT II

ACT III

ACT III SCENE I. LORD FRONTBOTHAM'S LODGINGS, NEXT DAY

[***LORD F*** IS RESTLESS, ***DELAFLOTE*** IS POTTERING AUDIBLY JUST OUTSIDE THE ROOM]

LORD F / (*calling*) Hey, man!
(*to self*) Man? That's debatable.

DELAFLOTE / (*off*) Meelord?

LORD F / (*calling*) Delaflote, bring my carriage to the door.

[***DELAFLOTE*** ENTERS THE ROOM]

DELAFLOTE / Carriage? Will your lordship venture to expose yourself so soon to the weather?

LORD F / I will venture as soon as I am able to expose myself to the ladies.

DELAFLOTE / I wish your lordship would please to keep to the house a little longer. I fear your lordship does not take the welfare of his wound into consideration.

LORD F / I will not be hiding away another day, even though I have as many wounds in my body as I have in my heart. Now deliver these invitations with all haste. This evening I shall visit my future father-in-law, Sir Tobias Coombs. I mean to commence my duties to the future Lady Fro'tham by entertaining guests at her father's expense.
And listen, tell Mr Lovelace I request the honour of his presence - and his impertinent wife - or I shall think we are not still friends.

DELAFLOTE / Oui, milord.

[EXIT ***DELAFLOTE***]

Act III Scene I. Lord Frontbotham's Lodgings, Next Day

LORD F / (*to self, arranging his dress in a mirror*) I'll visit my club first, then a good evening's merriment to help forget the pains of my near fatal wound. The ladies will be swooning at my feet when I show it to them, strike me speechless!

[ENTER *DELAFLOTE*]

DELAFLOTE / Milord, your sponge is here.

LORD F / Sponge? What the devil are you prattling on about, man?

DELAFLOTE / (*imitating wringing a sponge*) He squeeze you here, he squeeze you there.

LORD F / I'll squeeze your neck in a minute if you don't start talking sense! Explain yourself, man.

DELAFLOTE / You will see. (*calling*) Monsieur, Entrez!

[*TOM* ENTERS]

TOM / Brother, I am your servant.

LORD F / Oh, it's you, Tam.

DELAFLOTE / Shall I take your coat, sir? (*he takes Tom's jacket*) I shall give it to your handsome assistant to hold, I am sure he would enjoy that.

[*DELAFLOTE* EXITS WITH THE COAT]

TOM / Brother, I am your servant. How are you today?

LORD F / So well I have 'ardered' my carriage to the door. So there's no danger of death this day.

TOM / I'm very glad to hear it.

LORD F / That I don't believe 'far' a moment. Did your heart not jump into your 'mauth' when you heard I was run through the 'bady'.

TOM / Not that I recall, do you think it should have?

LORD F / I remember mine did when I heard my uncle was 'shat' in the head.

TOM / Only because he could no longer look after you financially.

LORD F / Well! 'naw' strike me dumb! He starved me. Starved me of a 'thousand' women, all for want of a 'thousand' pounds.

TOM / Then he saved you the expense of a great many cheap harlots.

LORD F / They were anything but cheap.

TOM / Then he did you a favour. I think any woman willing to take money is not worthy of it.

LORD F / If I were a younger brother I would think so too.

TOM / I presume you are seldom in love with these women.

LORD F / Never! strap my vitals!

TOM / Why then, did you make all this fuss about Amanda?

LORD F / Because she is a condescending woman of such irritating good virtue, I felt it my duty to corrupt her.

TOM / I see. And this is the type of person to have a fortune of ten thousand pounds a year.
Brother, I know talk of money is not so interesting a subject as talk of ladies, but the greatness of my needs is such that I hope you will have the patience to hear me out.

LORD F / The greatness of your needs, Tam, is the worst argument in the 'warld' for being patiently heard, and I do believe you are going to make a very good speech, but, - strike me dumb! – it has been the worst beginning of any speech I have heard this past twelve months.

Act III Scene I. Lord Frontbotham's Lodgings, Next Day

TOM / Then, in short; the expenses of my travels have exceeded my wretched annuity by such excess that I have been forced to mortgage it for five hundred pounds, which I've spent. So unless you are kind enough to assist me in redeeming it, I have no other option but to steal a purse.

LORD F / If I were you, 'Tam', I'd start planning your criminal career. Do you really think it reasonable I should give you five hundred 'paunds'?

TOM / I do not demand it as a right, brother, I am willing to receive it as a favour.

LORD F / You'd be willing to receive it any way it is given, strike me dumb! But these are damned hard times to give money in.

TOM / If you can't, I'll starve. It's as simple as that.

LORD F / Then all I can say is you should have been better husband material.

TOM / Damn you! If you can't live on ten thousand a year, how do you think I should do it on two hundred?

LORD F / My dear, 'Tam', I must remind you a race horse requires more looking after than a cart horse. Nature has made the same distinction between you and I.

TOM / A racehorse! You? Not only has nature addled your brain it has blinkered your eyes too. I truly wonder sometimes if you weren't muddled at birth with another baby and it was you dropped on your head not me.

LORD F / Don't be so passionate, 'Tam', for passion is the most unbecoming thing in the 'warld' to see. Nature made something of one of us and not the other.

TOM / Yes, she has made you older - curse her!

LORD F / That is not all, 'Tam'.

TOM / Why, what else is there?

LORD F / *(smug)* Ask the ladies.

TOM / You conceited dog! Do you think you have any advantage over me other than that which wealth has given you?

LORD F / It's not just the size of the purse that's important to a lady, 'Tam', and if I remember correctly you were lacking in all areas important to a lady.

TOM / That does it! Will you give me the money?

LORD F / Over my dead body.

TOM / With pleasure! Draw a sword, coward!

[**TOM** DRAWS A SWORD FROM A STAND]

LORD F / Why does everyone keep swords in Scarborough? Look Tam, you know I have always thought of you as a mighty dull fellow, and now you surpass yourself with one of the most foolish acts I have seen in a long time.

TOM / Face me, if you truly are a man!

LORD F / Does poverty make life such a burden, 'Tam', that you challenge me to a duel in the hope you run through my lungs and into my estate? Or failing that, I through yours to put an end to your pain?

TOM / Either way, I have nothing left to lose.

LORD F / Well, I will disappoint you in both your designs. So with the temperament of a 'philasapher' and the discretion of a diplomat, I leave the room with my blade untouched and my 'bady' unblooded.

[EXIT **LORD F**]

TOM / *(to self)* So! Farewell, brother. Now, my conscience is clear. *(calls)* Johnson!

[ENTER **JOHNSON**, EAGERLY]

Act III Scene I. Lord Frontbotham's Lodgings, Next Day

JOHNSON / (*eager*) Sir?

TOM / I have some news.

JOHNSON / Yes?

TOM / His lordship has given me a pill.

JOHNSON / A pill?

TOM / A pill to purge me of my scruples.

JOHNSON / You are going for the fortune then, sir?

TOM / I am. So quickly, run to the inn and get the carriage ready. Bring it to meet me at Dame Cummins' without delay. Now be gone, Johnson, fly!

JOHNSON / (*leaving at speed*) The happiest day I ever saw! I soar like a bird already. (*lower*) At last perhaps, I'll get my wages.

ACT III SCENE II. LOVELACE'S LODGINGS.

[*SOPHIA* ENTERS FROM A WALK REMOVING HER COAT]

WITHERS ENTERS BEHIND HER. *SOPHIA* HANDS HER COAT TO *WITHERS* WHO HANGS IT ON THE COAT STAND]

Sophia / It's certainly true what they say about the air in Scarborough.

Withers / Invigorating, madam?

Sophia / Bracing.

Withers / As you say, madam.

Sophia / A brisk stroll in the sea air certainly gets the blood flowing to the extremities. I think I'll freshen up before lunch.

Withers / Will that be all, Ma'am?

Sophia / Thank you, Withers, yes.

[EXIT *WITHERS*]

Sophia / (*to self*) Then to lay the groundwork for my revenge. While Amanda entertains my suitor, I shall entertain her husband. As long as Mr Lovelace thinks he has an inkling of a chance with me, he will take the bait like a lamb to the slaughter. He is just a man, after all.

[EXIT *SOPHIA* THROUGH ONE DOOR]

[ENTER *LOVELACE* THROUGH ANOTHER FOLLOWED BY *WITHERS*. HE REMOVES HIS COAT AND HANDS IT TO *WITHERS* TO HANG ON THE COAT STAND]

Lovelace / Is my wife inside?

Withers / No, sir, she went out half an hour ago.

Lovelace / Good. Is Sophia in?

Act III Scene II. Lovelace's Lodgings

WITHERS / She will be down shortly I believe. Will that be all, sir?

LOVELACE / Yes. You may go.

[EXIT **WITHERS**]

LOVELACE / (*to self, as he pours a drink*) Why can't I get this young widow out of my mind! Never has my heart been so suddenly seized before. Of all the women my wife should chose as a playfellow!
But what fate brings, let fate answer for. I did not seek it, but I will pursue it with all my resolve. How could she resist my charms? She is but woman, after all... (*he raises his glass and drinks*)

[**SOPHIA** ENTERS INTERRUPTING **MR LOVELACE'S** THOUGHTS]

SOPHIA / Mr Lovelace.

LOVELACE / (*turning, surprised*) Ah, Sophia my dear. (*he kisses her hand*) Drink?

SOPHIA / A little early for me, so just a small one, I don't like to be squiffy before I get my feet under the table.

LOVELACE / (*pouring a drink*) One small one coming up.

SOPHIA / You looked rather thoughtful when I came in, Mr Lovelace. I hope you are not ill.

LOVELACE / I was just debating, madam, whether I was ill or not, hence my thoughtfulness. (*passes a drink to Sophia*)

SOPHIA / Is it so hard to decide? I thought everyone was acquainted with their bodies, though few people know their own minds, I find.

LOVELACE / What if the ailment I suspect, is of the mind?

SOPHIA / Then you are in luck. I am familiar with the effects a man's mind has upon his body, I have had cause to study the effects on a number of occasions.

LOVELACE / What would you recommend I do then?

SOPHIA / If you'd allow me to be your physician, I would prescribe you a cure.

LOVELACE / I fear this would only exacerbate the situation. Should I place myself in your hands I believe my ailment would only increase in magnitude.

SOPHIA / An interesting case, I may have to study my college books for the cure, but I'm sure I can ease the symptoms in the meantime.

LOVELACE / Ease them?

SOPHIA / I have healing hands.

LOVELACE / If I could be sure of it I would place myself at your mercy here and now.

SOPHIA / Whether you are sure of it or not, what risk is there in trying?

LOVELACE / You may betray my case to my wife.

SOPHIA / And lose my practice?

LOVELACE / You would swear to keep my secret?

SOPHIA / I swear by all mankind.

LOVELACE / Not by mankind, since the dawn of time woman has been untrue to man. Swear by something else.

SOPHIA / Very well, then I swear by all womankind!

Act III Scene II. Lovelace's Lodgings

LOVELACE / Good, I am satisfied. Now, listen to my symptoms and give me your diagnosis;
It started when I first saw you at a play, a random glance you threw captured me, I could not avert my eyes. As I gazed upon you my heart raced, my eyes burned, and the world around me spun as the blood rushed from my head. I had to flee to the shelter of Amanda's arms.

SOPHIA / And what relief did she offer you?

LOVELACE / Why, instantly the symptoms subsided, - but now again, since you appeared I feel my problem return, and so increased in magnitude that if you do not help me alleviate it, I will before your very eyes explode. Give me your hand.

[HE TAKES HER HAND PULLING HER TO HIM]

SOPHIA / (*pretend offence*) Mr Lovelace! Unhand me! You have a fever and I shall be infected too.

[SHE PULLS AWAY, THOUGH NOT CONVINCINGLY]

LOVELACE / [PULLING HER BACK TO HIM]
Good, then we can die together in each other's arms, my charming angel.

SOPHIA / The devil's gotten into you! Let me –
(*hissed*) Quick, someone's coming!

[ENTER **WITHERS**. THEY PART A FEW PACES, COMPOSING THEMSELVES]

LOVELACE / Yes? What is it, man?

WITHERS / Sorry to, erm, intrude, sir, but my lady has returned and desires to speak with you in the dining room.

LOVELACE / Tell my wife I am coming...

WITHERS / Sir.

[***WITHERS*** EXITS]

LOVELACE / (*to Sophia*) …with your lady's permission.

SOPHIA / With your wife's permission.

LOVELACE / I know what I meant.

SOPHIA / I know what you meant. Now, go, your wife is calling.

LOVELACE / Before I go, one taste of nectar to drink to her health.

[HE TAKES **SOPHIA**'S HAND AND PULLS HER TO HIM]

SOPHIA / Stand away, or I shall start taking a even greater disliking to you.

LOVELACE / In matters of love, a woman is as likely to say things she doesn't mean as a man, I find.

[HE KISSES HER]

SOPHIA / (*in weak protestation to his kiss and part enjoyment*) Umm!

[***COLONEL CHUMLEY*** APPEARS AT THE DOOR UNNOTICED BY THEM]

CHUMLEY / (*to self*) What's this? -- Sophia and Lovelace? -- And in such close circumstances!

LOVELACE / Adieu, sweet angel.

[EXIT ***LOVELACE*** HAPPILY THROUGH THE DOOR OPPOSITE ***COLONEL CHUMLEY***]

CHUMLEY / (*to self*) So! Now I understand her indifference to me! Devious woman!
Well then, let Lovelace look out for his wife, it would only be fair retaliation after all.

[***COLONEL CHUMLEY*** APPROACHES ***SOPHIA*** UNSEEN]

SOPHIA / (*to self*) Men are so weak.

CHUMLEY / (*approaching from behind*) Your servant, madam.

Act III Scene II. Lovelace's Lodgings

SOPHIA / (*surprised*) Oh! Colonel Chumley!

[HE TAKES AND KISSES HER HAND]

CHUMLEY / I need not ask how you are, you are positively blooming with colour.

SOPHIA / (*stand offish*) No more than before, I think.

CHUMLEY / A little more blood to your cheeks, perhaps?

SOPHIA / I have been taking a walk.

CHUMLEY / Wasn't that Mr Lovelace I saw just leaving?

SOPHIA / Oh, yes – he has been walking with me.

CHUMLEY / Is that what you call it. -Madam, may I, coming straight to the point, trouble you with a few serious questions?

SOPHIA / As many as you please, but if you could, Colonel, let them be as least serious as possible.

CHUMLEY / How long has it been now since you and I started keeping company?

SOPHIA / I don't know exactly, but it has been a tedious, long time.

CHUMLEY / Almost two years, madam, and did I not come to this place at your express request, and for no other purpose than the honour of meeting you – and after waiting a month in disappointment were you courteous enough to explain, or in any way apologise, for your behaviour?

SOPHIA / Oh, Heavens! Apologise for '*my*' behaviour? - So, my good, '*serious*', Colonel, have you anything more to add?

CHUMLEY / Nothing, madam, except that after this impertinence towards me, I am less surprised at what I saw just now. Do you think it proper that a woman who trifles with the attentions of an honourable lover should be found flirting with the husband of her good friend?

SOPHIA / No more proper than it was for that *'honourable lover'* to be found *'flirting'* with his *'good friend's'* wife! Oh Colonel, Colonel, don't talk to me of *'honour'* for heaven's sake.

CHUMLEY / Really, madam! I do not understand what you are talking about.

SOPHIA / Come, come, you saw I did not pretend to misunderstand you. - But here comes the good lady now, perhaps you would rather be left alone with her for an explanation.

[*AMANDA* ENTERS DEEP IN THOUGHT]

CHUMLEY / (*to Sophia*) Oh madam, this accusation is pure invention. And to prove how much you are mistaken, I will decline the happiness you propose, and beg your leave. Madam, your servant.

SOPHIA / Colonel. Parting is such sweet pleasure.

[**COLONEL CHUMLEY** TURNS AND LEAVES. AS HE PASSES **AMANDA** HE WHISPERS SOMETHING IN HER EAR. SHE IN RETURN LAUGHS LIGHTLY AND AFFECTIONATELY AND WHISPERS SOMETHING BACK]

SOPHIA / (*sarcastically to self*) How tenderly they meet!
(*aloud to Amanda*) So, cousin, I hope you have not been reprimanding your admirer for being with me? I assure you we were talking about you.

AMANDA / Really, Sophia! My admirer! Do you ever talk seriously?

SOPHIA / Is something troubling you, Amanda? You appeared deep in thought when you entered.

AMANDA / I'm not sure. I've just left Mr Lovelace, perhaps it is nothing, but I detect a change about his manner which alarms me.

SOPHIA / What do you expect from a husband? I've never known a husband behave in a way which didn't alarm his wife.

AMANDA / But this is a sudden change, in the last day.

Act III Scene II. Lovelace's Lodgings

SOPHIA / I had not noticed any change.

AMANDA / That is because you've only been here a day, Sophia.

SOPHIA / My, doesn't time fly! Anyway, I have a simple answer to a husband's behaviour I recommend you try.

AMANDA / Which is?

SOPHIA / Caring as little for my husband as he does for me.

AMANDA / I can't help but care for my husband, Sophia, I love him so dearly.

SOPHIA / Look, Amanda, you can build castles in the sky, and fume and fret till you're old and grey, but I tell you, no man worth having is ever faithful to his wife, or ever was, or ever will be. Should temptation seek him he will chase it with gleeful abandon, - even more so if that offered is not available at home.

AMANDA / I am sure I fulfill his needs in every way I can. What more can I do?

SOPHIA / My dearest, Amanda, if you had wanted a faithful husband you should have chosen one who is kind but has no desirable manly qualities.

AMANDA / You think he is unfaithful to me?

SOPHIA / Think so? I am sure of it.

AMANDA / You are sure of it?

SOPHIA / Positive. He fell in love at the theatre.

AMANDA / Yes he mentioned it. But who could have told you this?

SOPHIA / Who told me? (*quickly thinking of a way out*) Why, the Colonel just now. I suppose your husband has made him his confidant.

AMANDA / Oh you lowlife, Lovelace!
(*a little too interested*) And what did the Colonel have to say on the matter?

SOPHIA / Say? Well, being a gentleman, he bitterly rebuked your husband of course, and reminded him of all the tender wonderful attributes you have and how he himself would desire nothing more in life than to have a woman such as yourself.

AMANDA / He did? Oh, my heart! I'm not feeling so well. Do excuse me, Sophia, I need to lie down.

[*AMANDA* TURNS AND EXITS THE ROOM]

SOPHIA / (*to self, after the departing Amanda*) Yes, but in whose bed, my dear, sweet, 'innocent' Amanda.

END OF ACT III

INTERMISSION

ACT IV

ACT IV SCENE I. OUTSIDE MUDDY MOAT HALL

[*TOM* AND *JOHNSON* ARE STANDING BEFORE A LARGE, REMOTE, RAMBLING COUNTRY HOUSE. THE HOUSE OF *SIR TOBIAS COOMBS* - MUDDY MOAT HALL.]

TOM / So this is our inheritance, Johnson, if we can just get possession of it. But I do rather think the seat of our family looks like Noah's Ark, as if it was chiefly designed for the fowls of the air and the beasts of the field.

JOHNSON / Sir, may I suggest we try not to distract your mind by dwelling on the architecture of the building. Go get the heiress, that's what we came for, let the devil take the house.

TOM / Get the house, I say! Let the devil take the heiress. -But come, we have no time to waste, knock at the door, Johnson.

JOHNSON / As you say, sir.

[*JOHNSON* KNOCKS AT THE DOOR AND WAITS]

TOM / What the devil? Have they no ears in this house? Knock harder.

[*JOHNSON* FINDS A STICK AND KNOCKS VERY LOUDLY ON THE DOOR]

TOM / Stop. Someone's coming.

TUMMOUS / (*within, strong country accent*) Who's there?

JOHNSON / Open the door and see. Is this your country manners?

TUMMOUS / I'll give you country manners! Ralph, load thy shotgun!

TOM / Oons! Try to say something nice, Johnson, or we'll be shot before we get so much as a glimpse of the fortune.

JOHNSON / (*loud through the closed door*) Hello? Mr Whatever-your-name-is-country-person? Will you let us in please?

TOM / (*rebuking*) Johnson!

[*JOHNSON* JUMPS LIKE A SCOLDED SCHOOLBOY, THEN JUMPS AGAIN AS A WINDOW OPENS AND A SHOTGUN IS POKED OUT OF IT]

TUMMOUS / Well 'naw', this 'ere gun I be a-'olding in me 'ands, wants to know - what's ya're business?

TOM / Nothing more, sir, than to wait upon Sir Tobias, see to it now.

TUMMOUS / To 'weat' upon Sir Tobias! Why, you'll find that's just the way Sir Tobias likes it. But how long you gonna be 'weating' around? I can't stand here all day talking to 'yous'

TOM / (*forced politeness*) My dear sir, would you be so kind as to do me the favour of asking Sir Tobias whether he pleases to see us or not?

TUMMOUS / Why, that's better, do yee see what a few nice words can do? (*calling to within*) Ralph, go thy ways, and ask Sir Tobias if he pleases to be waited upon – and hark ye – let Nurse know so she may lock up Miss Helen before the door is opened.

[THE WINDOW CLOSES AND IS LOCKED, FOOTSTEPS, MUFFLED BANGS, SHOUTS AND OTHER NOISES ARE HEARD FROM WITHIN]

TOM / Did you hear that, Johnson?

JOHNSON / Sir, with that thing pointing at me, he had my undivided attention.

TOM / Do you think they ever open this door? Even to come out and breed? I am becoming a little concerned at how high my intended wife can count on her two hands and three feet.

Act IV Scene I. Outside Muddy Moat Hall

[THE DOOR FLIES OPEN AND **SIR TOBIAS COOMBS** STANDS WITH SHOTGUN IN HAND. TUMMOUS STANDS BEHIND HIM]

TOBIAS / (*Bellows*) Who is it disturbing my peace?

JOHNSON / Oh!

[***JOHNSON* RUNS BEHIND *TOM***]

JOHNSON / (*to self*) Pray God they didn't hear what he just said. Oh, Lord! If they did we are both dead!

TOM / Johnson, you fool! Your fear will ruin us.

TOBIAS / Well, sir? Who is it that has any business with me?

TOM / Sir, it is I, if your name is Sir Tobias Coombs.

TOBIAS / Sir, my name is Sir Tobias Coombs, whether you have any business with me or not. So you see, I am not ashamed of my name, nor my face for that matter.

TOM / Sir, you have no cause to be, that I know of.

TOBIAS / Sir, if you have no cause to be either, then I desire to know who you are, for, until I know your name, I shan't be asking you into my house, and when I do know your name, it's six to four I shan't be asking you then.

TOM / My good sir, I hope you find this letter a suitable passport to your realm.

[***TOM* GIVES THE LETTER TO *TOBIAS* WHICH HE OPENS AND READS**]

TOBIAS / Upon my life! From Dame Cummins! I ask you lordship's pardon, ten thousand times over.
(*to Tummous*) Quickly man, run indoors, light the fire in the parlour. And be sure to air the room with some laurel.

TUMMOUS / Yes, sire.

[***TUMMOUS*** EXITS INSIDE]

TOBIAS / (*to Tom*) My lord, I ask your lordship's pardon.
(*Calling within*) And Tummous, tell Nurse to let Miss Helen loose again.
(*to Tom*) I hope your honour will excuse the disorder of my family, we do not receive men of your lordship's great quality every day. But, where are your carriages and your servants, my lord?

TOM / Sir, so I might give you and your daughter proof of how impatient I am to be closer related to you, I left my entourage to follow me, and came away post-haste with only the one servant.

TOBIAS / Your lordship honours me too much by exposing yourself to such danger and fatigue, I insist you do, but I promise you, sir, my daughter will endeavour to make whatever amends she can, and, though I should not say it myself, Miss Helen does have her charms.

TOM / Sir, I am no stranger to them, though I am to her of course, it is but common knowledge that she is one of the world's more beautiful and accommodating creatures.

TOBIAS / Aye, that she is, my lord, I am common knowledge's very grateful and humble servant. Now my lord, I want you to remember, my girl is young, but I have to say this for her, what she lacks in the arts, she makes up for in her breeding.

TOM / Something I am very much looking forward to.

TOBIAS / Oh, I can assure you, sir, she can be the most open and pleasing young thing when she puts her mind to it.

TOM / Really? - And she has her own mind too, you say?

TOBIAS / Pray, walk in, my lord, walk in.

ACT IV SCENE II. A BEDCHAMBER IN MUDDY MOAT HALL

[*MISS HELEN* IS ALONE LOCKED IN HER ROOM TALKING TO A STUFFED TOY]

HELEN / What do you think, Mr Biggy, my furry friend? I'm sure no one was ever treated the way I am! Locked in my room again. I know well enough what other girls do. It's just as well I have a husband coming or I would run off and marry the baker, so I would! Anybody knocks at the door and I have to be locked up, yet I can run loose about the house all day like a greyhound otherwise. Very nice!

[SOUND OUTSIDE DOOR OF STRUGGLE TO UNLOCK IT AND THEN *NURSE* BURSTS IN]

NURSE / Miss Helen! Miss, Miss, Miss Helen!

HELEN / Well, what's all the noise for, eh, nurse? Why do you pain my ears so? Can't a caged person get some peace around here?

NURSE / Peace? Someone has come that'll give you a 'piece' of something all right.

HELEN / Oh no, not Great Uncle Claude again. Anyway, why should I care a fig who comes or goes in this house while I am locked up like the wine in the cellar.

NURSE / That, young miss, is to prevent you being picked before you were ripe.

HELEN / Oh, don't you worry your head about that, I'm as ripe as you are, though not so wrinkled of course. In fact I'd probably say you were a little over-ripe.
(*preening before the mirror*) Look at me. I am a peach to your prune.

NURSE / Really! I have a good mind to lock you up again and not let you see your lord this evening.

HELEN / My lord?
(*excited*) Has my husband come for me?

NURSE / See how your attitude changes when there is something you want - and a fine piece of manhood too.

HELEN / (*hugging nurse*) Oh my dear, Nurse, forgive me this once, and I'll never insult you again, honestly. If I do you can put me over your knee and give me a good hard spanking.

NURSE / If you don't give me any more of your cheek, you may just find your 'husband' happy enough to take over that job from now on - if you're lucky.

HELEN / (*bouncing*) Dear nurse, don't lie to me now. Upon your honour, swear to me he has come.

NURSE / Upon my honour I couldn't say. But he is here. So you'd better start making yourself ready for him.

HELEN / Oh, Lord! I'll go put my lace evening dress on, though I'll probably be locked up like a monk for wearing it. And I don't think I'll be having any further need for you, Mr Biggy.

[SHE STUFFS THE TOY INTO A DRAWER AND KICKS IT SHUT WITH A SWIFT BACK HEEL]

NURSE / (*leaving*) Don't you want to know what he looks like?

HELEN / Who cares what he looks like. As long as he lasts till the end of the wedding ceremony I'll be free from all this.

NURSE / That's the truth, my angel, pray for a husband who can last!

[EXUENT]

Act IV Scene III. Lovelace's Lodgings.

[*AMANDA* AND *SOPHIA* ARE PRESENT. ENTER *WITHERS*]

WITHERS / Would ma'am be wishing me to lay out her jewellery?

AMANDA / (*agitated*) Yes. No. Oh, I don't know! Just leave me!

WITHERS / As you wish, ma'am.

[EXIT *WITHERS*]

SOPHIA / What in the name of Jove is the matter with you, Amanda?

AMANDA / The matter, Sophia? He plagues me to death, that's what.

SOPHIA / Who does?

AMANDA / Who do you think plagues a wife to death but her husband?

SOPHIA / Ah! So it has come to this. We'll have you wishing yourself a widow next.

AMANDA / I wish I were anything other than a wife right now. The low ungrateful man using me like this!

SOPHIA / I take it he has given you fresh reason to suspect his wandering.

AMANDA / Every hour gives me fresh reason.

SOPHIA / Then again, perhaps you cause the same doubts and jealousies in another's breast you so sorely feel in yours.

AMANDA / Heaven knows I would do no such thing.

SOPHIA / You haven't considered there may also be one tenderly attached to the one you boast as your conquest, Colonel Chumley?

AMANDA / Conquest? I'm sure I've never encouraged his advances.

SOPHIA / Pish, pish, Amanda! No sensible man ever pursues love without encouragement. Why haven't you behaved towards him as you did towards Lord Fro'tham?

AMANDA / Because he was not so forward. But let us drop the subject, it is the riddle of men's minds I wish to understand, not women's.

SOPHIA / Men are simple, Amanda. Remember how we played with our dolls when we were children. We were mad to have them as soon as we saw them, kissed them to pieces as soon as we held them, then we'd pull off their clothes and with all mystery removed, discard them again.

AMANDA / Well, what of it?

SOPHIA / That is how men see women.

AMANDA / Or perhaps some women see married men as an object to conquer and steal from a loving wife. My husband is following just such a flirt of a woman, though only for variety I suspect, I am sure he does not love her.

SOPHIA / You cannot know this for certain, Amanda.

AMANDA / Why? Do you know the ugly thing?

SOPHIA / I think I can guess at the person.
(*Preens her hair*) And she is no ugly thing either.

AMANDA / Is she pretty?

SOPHIA / Truly, I think so.

AMANDA / Whatever she is, I'm sure she's not pretty enough for him to enjoy anything more than a little light entertainment with.

SOPHIA / (*annoyed now*) Don't be too sure, Amanda. You have no right complaining that your husband is occupied elsewhere while you cause Colonel Chumley such suffering.

Act IV Scene III. Lovelace's Lodgings

AMANDA / Suffering? Me?

SOPHIA / Amanda, dear, you let him imagine there is hope by allowing his advances…

[*COLONEL CHUMLEY* COUGHS AT THE DOOR, PAUSES, THEN ENTERS]

SOPHIA / Talk of the devil.

AMANDA / I pray he did not hear our words.

CHUMLEY / Ladies, as I've come uninvited, I beg you, if I am intruding please feel free to turn me away.

AMANDA / No, no, Colonel, though my husband is not due home for some time - goodness knows what he is up to, but he spoke of accepting Lord Fro'tham's invitation to dine at Muddy Moat Hall this evening.

CHUMLEY / His lordship has been so kind as to honour me with an invitation too. If you'll allow me to escort you, I'll let you into a little secret as we go. In fact, both you ladies can play a part in it when we arrive.

AMANDA / (*cheerier*) Well, we have a couple of hours to spare yet. The carriages are not ordered till eight and it is only a five minute drive. -Cousin, let's keep the Colonel here with us till Mr Lovelace returns. Perhaps a few hands of whist?

SOPHIA / As you wish, Amanda, but as you know, I have an important letter I must write.

CHUMLEY / Madam, you know I would do anything you asked, but I am a wretched card player.

AMANDA / Oh, I'm sure you play well enough to lose your money, and that is all a lady requires in a man. My husband is up to no good I'm sure, and what's good for the goose is good for the gander, so without further ado, let us retire to the games room. A couple of glasses of wine and we'll see if we can't take that shirt off your back, eh, Colonel?
(*low to self*) And put a new dress on mine at last!

ACT IV SCENE IV. A ROOM IN MUDDY MOAT HALL

[ENTER *MISS HELEN*, NOW DRESSED IN HER LACE DRESS, AND *NURSE*]

NURSE / Well, miss, how did you like your husband to be?

HELEN / Oh Lord, Nurse, I am so overjoyed with him I can scarce contain myself!

NURSE / Oh, but you must be careful of being too fond. For a man nowadays, hates a woman to overly love him.

HELEN / Love him! What makes you think I love him, Nurse? Goodness, I would not care if he was hanged once I was married to him.

NURSE / I often wished my husbands had been well hung.

HELEN / (*oblivious to Nurse*) No, what makes me happy, is to think of what I'll be doing when I get to London. By golly, I'll flaunt it with the best of them when I'm a wife, and a lady too. And what's more, I'll have enough money to do so, Nurse.

NURSE / Ah, there's no knowing that, miss. These lords may have a power of wealth indeed, yet as I have heard say, they give it all to their sluts and their trollops - like leeches they are - whilst poor madam sits sighing and wishing with not a spare half-crown to her name.

HELEN / Oh, don't worry yourself about that, nurse, for my lord, I must say, is as free as an open house at Christmas. Why just this morning he told me I would have six hundred pounds a year pin money. Now if he gives me six hundred pounds a year to buy pins, just think how much he'll give me to buy petticoats.

Scarborough Fair (All's Fair In Love And Money)

NURSE / Oh my dearest, he deceives you most foully. That which they call 'pin money', is meant to buy everything in the world, right down to your very own under pinnings.
-But look, his honour is coming!
Now if I was sure you would behave yourself and not disgrace me – the one who brought you up – I'd leave you alone together.

HELEN / You have taught me, my good Nurse, to do unto others, as you'd have them do unto you.

NURSE / Yes, and this gives me cause for concern.

HELEN / Trust us together this once, and if I bring shame upon my breeding, may I never marry and may I die an old maid.

NURSE / Well, this once I'll let you – but if you let me down...!

HELEN / (*pushing Nurse*) Don't you worry, now be gone.

[***NURSE*** IS PUSHED OUT OF ONE DOOR AS ***TOM*** ENTERS ANOTHER]

TOM / My dear lady, I'm glad to find you alone for I have something important I wish to speak with you about.

HELEN / Sir – my lord, I meant – (*quick curtsey*) – you may speak with me about whatever you please, and I shall give a civil answer in return.

TOM / Very well, your father, I suppose you know, has made me a happy man by giving his consent to our marriage, I'm hoping I may obtain your consent in fulfilling his desires too.

HELEN / Sir, I never disobey my father in anything, -oh, except eating green gooseberries. I just can't swallow them. I don't know why with gooseberries, I have no problem with anything else.

TOM / Such traits in a daughter make for an admirable wife. I am impatient to make you mine, and hope you will consider the power of my love for you and not have the cruelty to delay my happiness for as long as your father had planned.

Act IV Scene IV. A Room In Muddy Moat Hall

HELEN / Why? When did my father say the marriage would be?

TOM / Madam, a lifetime away.

HELEN / (*shocked*) A lifetime?

TOM / Yes, a whole week.

HELEN / A whole week! Why, I shall be an old woman by that time.

TOM / And I, an even older man, which you'll find the greater misfortune.

HELEN / I thought it was going to be tomorrow morning as soon as I got up. I'm sure that's what Nurse told me.

TOM / And so it shall be! Tomorrow morning. If you'll consent.

HELEN / If I consent! Why, I thought I was to obey you as my husband.

TOM / That's when we are married. Till then I have to obey you.

HELEN / Why then, if we are to take it in turns it makes no difference. I'll obey you now, and when we are married you can obey me.

TOM / I think it best we stick to convention, but if we are to get married at all, first we must get the chaplain on our side.

HELEN / Have no fear about the chaplain. He loves my Nurse more than he loves preaching itself, and is always preaching to her about fulfilling his dreams with her.

TOM / Why then, my dear, if you'll call her here we'll try to persuade her right away.

HELEN / Oh Lord! I can tell you how to persuade her to do anything.

TOM / You can? How?

HELEN / Easy. Just tell her she is a fine, good looking woman. - Oh, and give her half a crown.

TOM / If that's all it takes she can have a dozen of them.

HELEN / Good Lord! For half that she'd marry you herself! I'll run and call her.

[*MISS HELEN* LEAVES]

TOM / So! Matters are going swimmingly. This is a rare girl indeed. I shall have a fine time with her in London.

[ENTER *JOHNSON* IN HASTE, LETTER IN HAND, LOOKING CONCERNED]

TOM / What is it, Johnson?

JOHNSON / Here, sir. I intercepted a note from the enemy. Your brother's porter brought it. I recognised him and pretended to be a servant.

[*JOHNSON* HANDS *TOM* THE LETTER. HE READS IT]

TOM / Egads! He tells Sir Tobias he'll be here this evening with a large party for supper! – I must marry the girl right away.

JOHNSON / Oh my goodness, not a moment to lose. - Here comes the girl now.

TOM / And the old Jezebel with her. Leave it to me, Johnson. You go.

[EXIT *JOHNSON* THROUGH ONE DOOR, ENTER *HELEN* AND *NURSE* THROUGH ANOTHER]

TOM / How do you do, good Mrs Nurse? -May I say, what an extremely fine looking woman you are. I swear, if I wasn't already promised, I would be joining the queue of beaus beating down the door for your favours.

NURSE / (*gives a bashful, flattered laugh*) Oh, sir! There in't no queue of beaus.

Act IV Scene IV. A Room In Muddy Moat Hall

TOM / You're probably wondering why I called for you. I asked your young lady to fetch you in order that I might thank you personally for your extraordinary care and kindly conduct in her upbringing. Pray accept this small token of my appreciation this moment, here…

[*TOM* GIVES A COIN FROM A PURSE TO *NURSE* WHICH SHE EXAMINES BOTH SIDES, BITES, THEN DROPS INTO HER CLEAVAGE FOR SAFE KEEPING]

NURSE / Thank'ee kindly, your lordship.

TOM / And you can depend on my further kindness at such a time as I become the happiest of men and marry this sweet young thing you raised so finely.

NURSE / Your lordship's kindness is too much, I'm sure. All I can boast is that I gave her pure and good milk from my ample breasts, as I am sure your lordship can see, and you should have seen how the poor thing thrived, and how she would look up from the teat and gurgle and laugh she would.

HELEN / (*taking Nurse angrily aside*) A word with you, Nurse. (*in confidence to Nurse*) I will ask you kindly, Nurse, to stop digging up old stories to make me ashamed in front of my love. Do you think such a fine and proper gentleman as he cares for trifling tales of a child? If you want him to have a good impression of a woman, don't tell him what she did then, tell him what she can do now.

[THEY RETURN FROM THEIR CONTRETEMPS]

HELEN / (*to Tom*) I hope your honour will excuse my ill manners of whispering in front of you. It was only to give orders about some family business.

TOM / Oh, everything, madam, must give way to business. Besides, good housekeeping is a commendable quality in a young lady.

HELEN / Tell me, sir. Are young ladies good housekeepers in London Town? Do they sew their own linen?

TOM / Oh no, they study how to spend money, not how to save it.

HELEN / Goodness. I don't know for certain, but I suspect that may be the better option.

TOM / Well, you can choose for yourself when you get there.

HELEN / Can I? Then by my honour, I'll get there as fast as I can. -Now, Nurse, his lordship enquires whether you'll be so good as to arrange for us to be married tomorrow.

NURSE / (taken aback) Tomorrow, madam?

TOM / My good lady, I can understand your surprise at Miss Helen's desire to put it off so long. Tomorrow! Pah! No, no, it's now, this very hour I would like the ceremony performed.

HELEN / Goodness, with all my heart I would like it too if it were at all possible.

NURSE / Mercy me! It gets worse and worse.

TOM / Yes, sweet Nurse, now and in private…here…

[*TOM* HANDS *NURSE* ANOTHER COIN, WHICH HAS THE DESIRED EFFECT OF SOFTENING HER]

NURSE / But if you get married now, what will you do when your father arranges for you to be married later?

HELEN / Why, then we shall be married all over again.

NURSE / Married twice, my child?

HELEN / Goodness, I don't care how often I get married, so long as I am married.

TOM / I pray, Nurse, that you would not deprive your young lady the pleasure of two wedding days…

[*TOM* HANDS *NURSE* A COIN]

TOM / (softer) …and of course, two wedding nights.

Act IV Scene IV. A Room In Muddy Moat Hall

[*TOM* HANDS *NURSE* A SECOND COIN]

HELEN / By jingo, yes! Two of everything I say!

NURSE / Much as it pains me to deny young lust the pleasure of two wedding nights...

[*TOM* HANDS OVER ALL THE REMAINING COINS IN A PURSE WHICH SHE ALSO STUFFS INTO HER DRESS CLEAVAGE AREA]

NURSE / ... I'm such a soft hearted fool, you shall be married this very evening.

HELEN / I shall? Oh Lord, I could jump for joy.

TOM / Dear Nurse, this goodness you show shall be further rewarded. But first we need to put to good use your persuasive powers over the chaplain to perform the ceremony. Do you think you can succeed with him?

NURSE / Succeed with him? If I don't he will never succeed with me agai... in future, I promise you that.

TOM / (*with a knowing smile*) And to strengthen your position with him, (*low, to Nurse*) horizontally or otherwise, (*aloud*) you can let him know that I have several fat incomes expected, and that the first to arrive shall be placed immediately at your disposal.

NURSE / (*quite excited now*) For that I could make him marry more than one couple, I promise you.

HELEN / Indeed do, Nurse. Make him marry you too. I'm sure he'd do it for a fat income, to match his fat living.

NURSE / I'd fatten him alright. I'd give him a good goosing and he could provide the sauce! (*laughs bawdily*)

TOM / Well, Nurse, while you go and settle matters with the chaplain, your lady and I will take a walk in the garden.

NURSE / Right you are, sir. I'm on my way.

[EXIT *NURSE*]

TOM / Come, madam. (*he offers her his arm*) Dare you venture out alone with me?

HELEN / (*taking his arm*) Oh yes, my lord. I don't think you could do anything with me I would find disagreeable.

TOM / (*low*) Better and better!

ACT IV SCENE V. SOPHIA'S DRESSING ROOM

[*LOVELACE* FURTIVELY ENTERS THE DARKENED ROOM]

LOVELACE / So far, so good. I've sneaked into the house unobserved and I find myself in Sophia's dressing room. What happy coincidence. What excuse can I use to show myself when she arrives? I believe she has shown me enough encouragement. – Wait, someone's coming. If it's my wife what the devil am I going to say? I don't think she trusts me as it is.

[SILHOUETTE OF A FEMALE WITH CANDLE OUTSIDE DOOR THROUGH GLASS. LOVELACE DARTS INTO THE WARDROBE LEAVING THE DOOR SLIGHTLY OPEN. SOPHIA ENTERS THE ROOM AND PREPARES HER WRITING IMPLEMENTS WITH HER BACK TO THE WARDROBE]

SOPHIA / (*to self*) What a situation! How he provokes me! I have lost all patience with the both of them. To think I have to sit and hear him compliment Amanda to my face! I've a good mind to let Mr Lovelace know how much they've moved me to a fit of temper.

[*LOVELACE* PEEKS FROM INSIDE THE DOOR. HIS DIM FACE EXPOSED IN THE DARKNESS]

SOPHIA / Yet I can't bear the thought of leaving them alone together. (*she starts undoing her clothing*) No, I'll change for dinner now and return. I'll have to do my letter writing later. I can't wait to see how disappointed that will make them…

[*SOPHIA* REMOVES HER DRESS. SHE NOW STANDS IN BASQUE AND STOCKINGS. *LOVELACE* ENJOYS THE SPECTACLE]

SOPHIA / I think I'll wear my daring number this evening. Show the old fool what he's missing.

[*SOPHIA* TURNS TO GET AN ITEM FROM THE WARDROBE, AS SHE DOES, *LOVELACE* PANICS AND DARTS BACK INSIDE THE WARDROBE AND IN DOING SO UPSETS ITEMS IN THE WARDROBE NOISILY. THE WARDROBE ROCKS. *SOPHIA* SCREAMS IN SHOCK]

SOPHIA / (*screaming*) Ahh! A Ghost! A Ghost!

[*LOVELACE* STAGGERS FROM THE WARDROBE, SHAKEN]

LOVELACE / Shh! Quiet, my angel! I'm not a ghost yet, but with that much noise I'll need some form of spirit to calm me.

SOPHIA / My God, sir! How dare you have the insolence to presume I...

WITHERS / (*off, within, concerned*) Madam?

SOPHIA / Quick, hide again. Someone's coming.

[*SOPHIA* PUSHES *LOVELACE* INTO THE WARDROBE AND LOCKS THE DOOR. *WITHERS* RUSHES INTO THE ROOM]

WITHERS / (*rushing in*) Is everything... (*eyes lighting up at the sight*) ...alright, madam, I heard a noise?

SOPHIA / (*grabbing her dress and holding it before her to protect her modesty*) Heavens! I'm almost frightened out of my mind.

WITHERS / Whatever happened?

SOPHIA / I, I thought I saw a ghost.

WITHERS / A ghost, madam? Where?

SOPHIA / Oh, er, I thought it was a ghost, but... (*she looks around, her eyes alighting on a cloak*) ...but it was just that black cape hanging on the stand. Yes that's what it was. I'm alright now. You can go. I am the most frightful fool.

WITHERS / As you wish, madam.

[*WITHERS* EXITS, LOOKING AT *SOPHIA* ODDLY]

Act IV Scene V. Sophia's Dressing Room

LOVELACE /   (*within cupboard*) Is the coast clear?

SOPHIA /   (*through the door to Lovelace*) The coast clear? Clear for what? Upon my word I wonder at your presumptions of me.

LOVELACE /   You wonder before I've had time to explain myself to you. -By the way, you handled Withers admirably.

SOPHIA /   (*flattered, but keeping a stiff demeanour*) I don't know why I allow myself to get into these situations.

[*LOVELACE* PUSHES ON THE DOOR. REALISING IT IS LOCKED, HE KNOCKS FROM WITHIN THE WARDROBE]

LOVELACE /   (*knocking*) Sophia? Unlock the door. It's a little difficult conversing through wood.

SOPHIA /   (*unlocking the door*) I really can't believe you men someti...

[*LOVELACE* BURSTS OUT FROM THE WARDROBE]

LOVELACE /   (*bursting out*) Where's my wife?

SOPHIA /   Playing cards.

LOVELACE /   With whom?

SOPHIA /   Colonel Chumley, why?

LOVELACE /   Then we are safe.

SOPHIA /   Safe? Some husbands would think differently if he were playing with their wives.

LOVELACE /   And they'd be right to think so, but I trust mine.

SOPHIA /   Really? And she, no doubt, has the same confidence in you, yet do you think she would be happy to find you here?

LOVELACE /   Egads, you're right! – We'd better go in the next room out of the way.

SOPHIA /   In the dark?

LOVELACE / If you wish.

SOPHIA / You are certainly very impudent.

LOVELACE / Me? No. Let me show you, my angel...

SOPHIA / You are very mistaken about 'your angel', I assure you.

LOVELACE / I hope not...(*taking her hand*) ...for by this hand I swear...

SOPHIA / Let go of my hand, or I shall take an even stronger disliking to you and I shall call out for help, believe me.

LOVELACE / Impossible! (*He pulls her to him, embracing her tightly*) You could not be so cruel to me.

SOPHIA / Hel...

[HE KISSES HER, SILENCING HER TOKEN ATTEMPT TO CALL FOR HELP. HE BREAKS THE KISS]

SOPHIA / (*softer*) Help me!

[HE KISSES HER AGAIN THEN PICKS HER UP IN HIS ARMS AND CARRIES HER THROUGH THE INNER DOOR]

SOPHIA / (*softly*) Help! Help!

[HE CLOSES THE DOOR BEHIND THEM]

[THERE IS A PAUSE WHERE WE CAN ONLY GUESS AS TO WHAT IS HAPPENING]

AMANDA / (*off, distant*) Sophia? ... Sophia?

[**SOPHIA** EMERGES FROM THE ROOM FRANTICALLY REARRANGING HERSELF]

SOPHIA / Someone is coming! Quickly, go.

LOVELACE / (*within*) I will stay here and wait for your return.

Act IV Scene V. Sophia's Dressing Room

SOPHIA / I will never trust myself in a room alone with you again as long as I live.

[*LOVELACE* EMERGES FROM THE ROOM WITHOUT HIS TROUSERS ON]

LOVELACE / But I have something I must share with you.

SOPHIA / So I can see! Get dressed. Quickly.

LOVELACE / When will I see you...

SOPHIA / Go! I take the air every day and return by seven. If you are fond of an evening sundowner you'll know where to find me.

LOVELACE / (*turning towards the door*) I am never one to disappoint a lady.

AMANDA / (*outside door*) Sophia? Are you in there, Sophia?

SOPHIA / (*hissed*) It's Amanda! Quickly. In there.

[*SOPHIA* GRABS HIM, FORCEFULLY THROWING HIM IN THE WARDROBE AND LOCKING THE DOOR]

SOPHIA / (*to self, locking the wardrobe door, grabbing her dress and stepping into it*) I hope she has not heard his voice. Though it would be only fair she had her share of jealousy in return. (*calling aloud*) In here, Amanda.

[*AMANDA* ENTERS THE ROOM]

AMANDA / Sophia, why did you leave me?

SOPHIA / I thought I spoiled your party.

AMANDA / Since you have been gone, Colonel Chumley has attempted improper behaviour. Heaven knows what would happen if my husband heard of his conduct.

SOPHIA / (*loudly for Lovelace to hear*) Oh no! Mr Lovelace must not hear of the Colonel's improper conduct under any circumstances.

AMANDA / (*puzzled at the loudness*) Oh no! Not for the world. Are you feeling all right, Sophia? You look a little flushed.

SOPHIA / I'm fine, Amanda, a little jealous perhaps of the attention you receive in my absence. But come, let us go back. I don't think I can trust leaving you two love birds alone together.

AMANDA / (*playful indignation*) Oh! Sophia!

[**AMANDA** & **SOPHIA** EXIT THE ROOM, LEAVING **LOVELACE** LOCKED IN THE WARDROBE]

LOVELACE / (*in wardrobe*) So! Fine behaviour from a wife! Colonel Chumley attempts to make love to my wife, and I am not to hear of it *'under any circumstances'*! I must ask her about this, and, by Heavens! if I find that Amanda has… - but wait… (*rattles the door trying to open it*) I'm a fine example to set. (*realizing it is locked*) I'm locked in a wardrobe. God forbid anyone finds me here.

[HE RATTLES THE DOOR FRUITLESSLY]

LOVELACE / Sophia?
Hello?
Anyone?

END OF ACT IV

ACT V

ACT V SCENE I. THAT EVENING IN LOVELACE'S LODGINGS

[*MR LOVELACE* IS WAITING ALONE IN THE DRAWING ROOM. A CLOCK CHIMES, MARKING SEVEN O'CLOCK. *LOVELACE* GLANCES AT IT IMPATIENTLY]

LOVELACE / Does she plan to make a fool of me? Have me stand here all evening? My wife will soon be enquiring after me to set out for our supping party.
I'll give her five more minutes. I'm missing my evening cocktail, and in my experience no woman on earth is worth putting before such…

[A DOOR BELL RINGS WITHIN]

LOVELACE / Ah, this will be her now… hopefully with a welcoming smile and an offer to compensate all the anxiety and suffering, not to mention the expense, of keeping a mistress.

[ENTER *SOPHIA*]

LOVELACE / Sophia, such a joy of light to behold in the darkness of my world.
(*he greets her with a kiss*)
Had you been five minutes later I… (*stops*)

SOPHIA / You would have gone, I suppose?

LOVELACE / Oh course not, my dear. How could you think such a thing?

SOPHIA / Well, I can assure you it is against my better judgment I came at all. I am beginning to think you too dangerous a being to trifle with.

LOVELACE / You cannot mean it, surely? Do you not find pleasure in my company?

SOPHIA / In your company, yes. But I'm concerned what *'pleasure'* you – a married man - expect from me?

LOVELACE / How doubly cruel of you to remind me of my misfortune!

SOPHIA / A misfortune to be married to so lovely a woman as Amanda?

AMANDA / *(calls, within)* Mr Lovelace! Where are you? I must speak with you.

LOVELACE / S'truth! Now look what you've done by speaking her name. She's here.

WITHERS / *(within)* I believe they are in the drawing room, madam.

AMANDA / They?

LOVELACE / Oops. We'd better get out of sight. I don't want to raise her suspicions any higher than they already are...

COLONEL / *(calling within)* Amanda?

LOVELACE / The Colonel too. Quickly. Hide. I'd like to learn more about what my wife gets up to behind my back that I *'shouldn't know for all the world'*!

[***LOVELACE*** SNEAKS BEHIND A SCREEN]

SOPHIA / I would disgrace womankind if I allowed myself to be outdone by a man when it comes to curiosity...

[***SOPHIA*** SNEAKS BEHIND A SECOND SCREEN. THE SCREENS ARE POSITIONED SO THAT WE CAN SEE THE PAIR HIDING BEHIND THEM AND OBSERVE THEIR REACTIONS TO THE WORDS SPOKEN]

[ENTER ***AMANDA***]

AMANDA / Mr Lovelace? Are you here?
-Oh bother, where did that man go.

[ENTER ***COLONEL CHUMLEY*** BEHIND AMANDA]

Act V Scene I. That Evening In Lovelace's Lodgings

CHUMLEY / Good evening, madam.

AMANDA / Oh, you again, Colonel. How persecuted I am.

CHUMLEY / Madam? You seem disturbed.

AMANDA / I have the best reason in the world to be disturbed - a husband. I really don't know quite what has become of him of late. He was found locked in a wardrobe earlier.

CHUMLEY / A wardrobe?

AMANDA / (*unconvinced*) He said he was looking for his trousers.

CHUMLEY / I can't say I'm surprised. However, I would gladly bear your pain and remove your malady, if Heaven and your good self would permit it of me.

AMANDA / Your interference would only add to my distress, Colonel.

CHUMLEY / *Au contraire*, madam, treat like with like. Realise the strength and beauty of your charms, rouse up that spirit of woman within – take a lover.

AMANDA / A lover? What nonsense do you speak of now, Colonel?

CHUMLEY / It is not nonsense, I speak with some considerable experience on the matter.

AMANDA / I am a married woman.

CHUMLEY / A married woman with a lover standing before her, with zeal enough to cure her sadness, and zest enough to fill her every desire.

AMANDA / Where?

CHUMLEY / Here of course! I speak of myself.

AMANDA / And what if Mr Lovelace were to hear of the offer you lay before me?

CHUMLEY / He is in no position to reprimand me if he did. In fact he deserves it from me.

AMANDA / Deserves it?

CHUMLEY / Yes, he has been as untrue in his love to you, as he has in his friendship with me.

AMANDA / With you?

CHUMLEY / Yes, madam. The lady with whom he now deserts these – (*looking her up and down approvingly*) delectable charms - was mine by right, and I believe inclination too. Yes, Madam Sophia, who now...

AMANDA / (*interrupting*) Sophia!?

LOVELACE / (*low grimacing*) Oons!

AMANDA / Impossible!

CHUMLEY / Yes, Sophia, who...

AMANDA / I refuse to believe it.

CHUMLEY / I assure you it is true, I speak with the conviction of a man who has seen it with his own eyes. Why, this very day I saw them together and...

AMANDA / Silence, sir! I will not listen to such slander – This is a poor device to weaken my defences. No, sir, Mr Lovelace may be capable of certain misjudgments in his actions from time to time...

LOVELACE / (*mouths*) Misjudgments?

AMANDA / ...however, you should have chosen a more believable person for my rival. Sophia is my relation and a good, close friend.

SOPHIA / (*hissed*) You tell the old lech, Amanda!

CHUMLEY / If I do not prove to you...

Act V Scene I. That Evening In Lovelace's Lodgings

AMANDA / (*interrupting*) ...You shall not have the chance. From your words just now I might have been misled – if I had believed what you said to be true – to have offered you a little comfort, and I believe now this was your devious plan. But this one last ungentlemanly deception is worthy of my full resentment and contempt. I have never given my husband any reason to doubt my love and commitment to him, and nor shall I in future, especially, Colonel, with you. I therefore bid you goodbye.

[*AMANDA* STORMS OFF]

CHUMLEY / (*to self*) She has spirit, I'll say that for her. – But can I bear to lose Sophia without revenge of some form, or compensation at least? ... I'm not willing to share her with another man ... Perhaps I do love her after all. -Wait! Did I just utter the L-word? Hie thee to the medicinal cabinet, Chumley, old boy! A stiff one before you lose your senses completely and start uttering the M-word!

[*COLONEL CHUMLEY* LEAVES WITH A PURPOSE]

[*LOVELACE* AND *SOPHIA* EMERGE FROM HIDING]

LOVELACE / I could do with a drink too.

SOPHIA / It came as a bit of a shock did it? A taste of your own medicine? So, what do you have to say?

LOVELACE / In truth, I hardly know what to say.

SOPHIA / What about us now?

LOVELACE / Us? I believe we should probably stop.

SOPHIA / (*pretence of indignation*) We! Why you monster, you don't pretend that I ever entertained such a thought?

LOVELACE / In all honesty, Sophia, my wife's behaviour just then touched me. I have made certain errors of judgment in the past I admit, and she has always stood by me throughout, but these last couple of days I've witnessed the shoe on the other foot.

SOPHIA / There is nothing like another man showing interest, to make a wife interesting to her husband once again.
Will you tell Amanda she has just cause to be interested in her husband's behaviour earlier?

LOVELACE / There is no need, nothing has happened between us, Sophia... yet.

SOPHIA / And nor will it ever, Mr Lovelace. My trifling with you was no more than a foolish attempt to make the Colonel jealous, and I now believe there is a similar motive behind his actions. Amanda's words just then touched my heart. Perhaps there is something in old fashioned, romantic love after all. So, you can depend on me making no mystery of the matter with him.

[*AMANDA* ENTERS UNSEEN BY THE COUPLE. SHE STOPS TO OBSERVE AND LISTEN]

LOVELACE / I beg you not to tell the Colonel about you and I, Sophia.

[*AMANDA* GASPS, SHOCKED, PUTTING HER HAND TO HER MOUTH]

LOVELACE / In return I am willing to overlook his conduct.

SOPHIA / His conduct?

LOVELACE / Yes, or how will he be able to look me in the face again?

SOPHIA / How will you be able to look him in the face again?

LOVELACE / He dared to take the honour of my wife!

SOPHIA / And you dared to take the honour of his mistress!
Come, come. Don't pretend your behaviour was any better than his, or my virtue any less than hers.

AMANDA / (*low to self, shocked*) The Colonel was telling the truth!

LOVELACE / Perhaps, but don't forget, *'Flattery makes friends, while truth makes enemies'*

Act V Scene I. That Evening In Lovelace's Lodgings

SOPHIA / Ah, but my good, Mr Lovelace, *'The truth will always out'*. So, in this case, better out than in, as they say, don't you think?

LOVELACE / Not quite the wording I would have chosen.

> [***LOVELACE* AND *SOPHIA* LAUGH AND EXIT TOGETHER, ARMS LINKED, UNAWARE *AMANDA* OVERHEARD THEM**]

AMANDA / (*coldly*) So the merry widow was right after all, I am an old fashioned, romantic fool to believe in true love ever after. But not any more. Just you wait, Mr Lovelace, you'll see.

ACT V SCENE II. THAT EVENING IN MUDDY MOAT HALL

[*NURSE*, *MISS HELEN*, AND *TOM* ENTER]

TOM / My good Nurse, I'll be forever in your debt, as long as you live.

HELEN / And mine too, I promise you.

NURSE / I most humbly thank your good selves. May your children swarm about you like bees to a honeycomb.

HELEN / I wish this with all my heart – the more the merrier I say, eh Nurse?

[*JOHNSON* ENTERS LOOKING EARNEST]

JOHNSON / A word with you, sir, it's rather urgent.

TOM / What the devil's the matter, Johnson?

[*TOM* AND *JOHNSON* STAND ASIDE IN CONFIDENCE]

JOHNSON / Sir, your brother has arrived, with two coaches, six horses, twenty footmen, and a fancy coat worth enough to part even the coldest of lips – so you be the judge of where your ladies heart may choose to be directed.

TOM / Egads, is he in the house yet?

JOHNSON / No, they are holding him at the gate. Luckily, Sir Tobias takes him for an impostor - I told him I had heard of just such a plot before.

TOM / Perfect!
(*turning to Miss Helen*) My dear, my man has told me of a troublesome business, but do not be alarmed, we are made of sterner stuff than this rogue.

HELEN / Rogue? What rogue?

Act V Scene II. That Evening In Muddy Moat Hall

TOM / An impudent fellow has arrived at the gate not realising I was already here, and has assumed my name in the hope of running away with you, my dear.

HELEN / With me?

TOM / Yes my dear, how preposterous is that.

HELEN / Why the brazen faced varlet! It's just as well you arrived when you did, I might have married the wrong man had he arrived earlier.

TOM / You are more right than you can imagine.
-Nurse, run to Sir Tobias and stop him from going to the gate until I've had a word with him.

NURSE / If it pleases your honour, perhaps my lady and I should lock ourselves away until the danger has passed.

TOM / Hmm, yes. Perhaps it would be for the better.

HELEN / Not so fast. I won't be locked up any more, not now I have a husband come for me!

TOM / Yes, my dear, but I ask that you do it this once until we have seized the rascal.

HELEN / No, not if you ask me. But if you order me as your wife I will obey you in anything.

TOM / (*low, agreeably*) Hmm, better and better!
(*sternly*) Go with the Nurse, I will come for you when it is safe.

HELEN / (*excited at the danger and being ordered*) Oh yes, my lord.

[***MISS HELEN*** SCAMPERS OFF WITH ***NURSE***]

TOM / Listen, Johnson, the situation is better than you imagine.

JOHNSON / The devil it is, sir, we'll have to flee.

TOM / Calm down. All we have to do is brazen this business out and turn the role of imposter over to his lordship, which knowing my brother, may not be such a difficult task.

[ENTER **SIR TOBIAS**, HIS VOICE BOOMING, **JOHNSON** REACTS WITH A START]

TOBIAS / Ah, there you are, my lord.

TOM / (*turning to Tobias*) Did you ever hear of such impudence, sir?

TOBIAS / Never, in all my life! But we'll show him the Coombs' are not to be trifled with, I can assure you.

TOM / I have heard, sir, he has a great many people with him disguised as servants.

TOBIAS / Aye, rogues. But we have mastered them. We fired a few shots over their heads and they scurried away in an instant. (*Calls out*) Tummous. Bring in our prisoner.

TOM / Wait! - If you please, sir. - I have an idea it will be best for me not to confront this fellow yet. You can then hear from him exactly what his intentions are and how far he hopes to push his luck with them.

TOBIAS / Your lordship is a genius! My lord, please step aside then while I handle this.

TOM / With pleasure, sir.

JOHNSON / (*low, sarcastically*) What masterful modesty my master has.

[**TOM** AND **JOHNSON** EXIT THROUGH A SIDE DOOR]

TOBIAS / (*calls*) Come, come. Bring him in.

[**TUMMOUS** MANHANDLES **LORD F** INTO THE ROOM]

LORD F / What the plague do you mean by this gentlemen? Am I to assume you are all drunk before supper?

Act V Scene II. That Evening In Muddy Moat Hall

TOBIAS / Drunk, sir! You are an impudent rogue. Drunk or sober, I am a Justice of the Peace and know how to deal with drifters like you.

LORD F / Drifter?

TOBIAS / Aye, drifter, vagabond. Now give an account of yourself. What's your name? Where do you live? Do you pay taxes?

LORD F / Why are you asking me so many impertinent questions?

TOBIAS / I'll have you answer them before I am done, you rascal!

LORD F / As God is my witness, the only answer I can give to them is that you are a very extraordinary old fellow, strap my vitals! (*he laughs*)

TOBIAS / So, you think this is funny, do you? I will show you we know how to deal with your sort.
(*to Tummous*) Draw up a warrant for his arrest immediately.

TUMMOUS / Yes, sir. Right away, sir.

[***TUMMOUS* EXITS**]

LORD F / A warrant? What the devil are you aiming at, old man?

TOBIAS / I would be aiming at you, sir, if my hands were not tied as a magistrate. And with these two fists be beating your teeth down your throat, so help me!

LORD F / And for what reason do you feel this desire to spoil my face?

TOBIAS / For your designs to steal my daughter, sir!

LORD F / Steal your daughter? Now I understand! I am asleep in bed and this is all one big dream. Pray, father, will you at least answer me one question?

[***TUMMOUS* RE-ENTERS WITH PAPERWORK**]

TOBIAS / I can't say whether I will or not until I hear the question.

LORD F / Then here is my question. Did you or did you not, write to Lord Fro'tham asking him to come and marry your daughter?

TOBIAS / No sir, I did not. I did, however write to Lord Front-bottom, and he has come and shall marry my daughter before she is another day older.

LORD F / (*sighs at the pronunciation*) Then give me your hand, father, we understand one another at last!

TOBIAS / The fellow is completely mad! Tie him hand and foot.

[***TUMMOUS* FORCEFULLY TIES *LORD F* TO A CHAIR**]

LORD F / (*struggling as he is tied*) Enough of this fooling. Your joke is growing dull.
(*to Tummous*) Get off me!

TOBIAS / Hold him tight. Tie him up I say, he's quite mad. We'll see if bread and water, a dark room, and a whip won't bring him to his senses.

LORD F / Egad, if I don't wake up soon, this is likely to prove the most disturbing dream of my entire life.
-I beg you, tell me why you take such offence at my introduction that you feel the need to pin my limbs like a trapped rabbit.

[ENTER *MISS HELEN* AND *NURSE*]

[*TUMMOUS* EXITS]

HELEN / (*going up to Lord F*) Hello father. Is this the man who would have run off with my innocence?
Phew! How he stinks of perfume! I pray you let him be dragged through the horse pond, father.

LORD F / (*sarcastic*) So this must be my wife, judging from her inclination to naturally support her husband in his hour of need.

Act V Scene II. That Evening In Muddy Moat Hall

HELEN / Silence, rogue. What do you intend to do with him, father? Hang him?

TOBIAS / That, at least, my child.

NURSE / Aye, and even that's too good for him.

HELEN / You said hanged men were good for marriage earlier, Nurse.

NURSE / You'll learn my meaning soon enough, young miss.

LORD F / And you must be the governess I presume. From what I see this appears to be the most extraordinary of families that a man was ever matched into.

TOBIAS / A family you'll wish you never trifled with. What has become of his lordship, daughter?

HELEN / He's just coming, father.

LORD F / Coming? Does no one see me? What on earth is going on here?

[*TOM* AND *JOHNSON* ENTER THE ROOM]

TOBIAS / Ah, here he is now, welcome your lordship.

LORD F / Strap my vitals! 'Tam'! Now at last the dream can cease!

TOM / Is this the fellow who designs to trick me out of your daughter, sir?

TOBIAS / That he is, my lord. How do you like that, eh? A rogue trying to trick his way into my family and my pockets!

TOM / I hope he is not foolhardy enough to expect much in the way of favour from me.

LORD F / Strike me dumb, 'Tam', you are an impudent fellow!

TOBIAS / You impertinent scoundrel! Where do you think you are man? A public alehouse? Address his lordship correctly!

LORD F / (*sarcastically*) My dear 'Lord', may I beg one word in confidence with your lordship?

NURSE / Ha! It's lord he calls him now! See how bondage humbles even the craftiest of rogues. I know whenever I'm... (*she stops*) ...oh, no, it was something else I was thinking of. (*laughs nervously*)

[**TOM** APPROACHES **LORD F**]

HELEN / I pray you do not get too close, my lord, lest he bites off your ear giving you his 'one word'.

LORD F / I am not altogether as hungry as your ladyship presumes to imagine.
(*in confidence to Tom*) Look here, Tam, I am a sensible man, I know I haven't been so kind to you as perhaps I ought. So let's forget what's in the past, and let's say you accept my offer of five thousand 'paunds', and we'll say no more about it.

TOM / (*to Lord F in confidence*) It's far easier to prevent a disease than to cure it. A quarter of that sum would have secured your mistress, twice as much cannot redeem her.

TOBIAS / Well? What does he say?

TOM / The rascal had the damn cheek to offer me a bribe to let him go.

TOBIAS / Aye, and he should go, but with a plague on him! I'll call a constable so he can be taken away and locked up.

LORD F / (*disbelief*) Locked up?

[**TUMMOUS** ENTERS]

TUMMOUS / Sir, there be a Muster Lovelace and a Muster Colonel Chumley with some ladies at t'door.

TOBIAS / By the devil, what is going on today! Who?

TUMMOUS / Muster Lovelace and Must...

Act V Scene II. That Evening In Muddy Moat Hall

TOBIAS / (*interrupting*) Yes, yes, I heard you the first time, but who the devil are they?

TOM / A few invited friends I wish to introduce you to, Sir Tobias.

TOBIAS / Very well, show them in.

TUMMOUS / Sir.

[*TUMMOUS* EXITS]

LORD F / Strike me speechless! these are my invited guests, as they will soon inform you. Then we shall see who is the true, Lord Fro'tham!

JOHNSON / (*low to Tom*) Grief! What will you do now, sir?

TOM / (*low to Johnson*) Fear not, Johnson, all is not yet lost.

[*CHUMLEY, LOVELACE, AMANDA* AND *SOPHIA* ENTER]

LORD F / Thank goodness! Colonel Chumley, my good man, tell these people who I am.

[*CHUMLEY* IGNORES *LORD F* AND WALKS UP TO *TOM*]

CHUMLEY / (*to Tom, shaking his hand*) My lord, we are fortunate to be witness to your lordship's happiness.

TOM / Good to see you, gentlemen. You are welcome company indeed.

LORD F / (*in disbelief*) What the devil?
Lovelace. You'll vouch for me at least.

LOVELACE / My lord. (*bowing to Tom*) Will your lordship do the honour of introducing us to Sir Tobias?

TOM / With pleasure.

AMANDA / And of course to your good lady-to-be, sir.

LORD F / Gad take me. They're all in on the plot!

TOBIAS / Gentlemen, I am honoured to make the acquaintance of his lordship's friends, you will ever be offered welcome by me and mine.

TOM / (*to Helen*) My love, let me introduce you to these ladies.

HELEN / By golly, they look so fine and proper, I am almost ashamed to approach them.

AMANDA / A most engaging young lady indeed!

HELEN / (*curtseys*) Thank ye, ma'am.

LOVELACE / But, Lord Fro'tham...

LORD F / Sir!

LOVELACE / (*to Lord F angrily*) I was not addressing myself to you, sir! -- Pray who is this gentleman? He seems to be in a peculiar predicament.

TOBIAS / Ha! ha! Ha! So these are your friends and guests, eh, my precious adventurer?

LORD F / I am struck dumb by their impudence.

TOBIAS / This modest gentleman, only wanted to pass himself off as a Lord in order to carry off my daughter.

LOVELACE / A likely plot to succeed, truly it was. (*he laughs*)

LORD F / As God be my judge, Lovelace, I did not expect this of you. I beg you, confess the joke. Tell Sir Tobias I am the real Lord Fro'tham who yesterday attempted to make love to your wife, and in return was honoured with a box round the ears from her and then run through the body by your own good self.

TOBIAS / A likely story that a peer of the realm should behave like this.

LOVELACE / A pretty thick fellow who chooses to scandalize the character he wishes to assume. What will you do with him, Sir Tobias?

Act V Scene II. That Evening In Muddy Moat Hall

TOBIAS / Have him arrested and charged of course. He will be sentenced and dealt with by the full weight of the law - unless the bride and groom choose not to press charges, which is hardly likely to happen.

LORD F / Bride and groom! For Gad's sake, 'tis 'tarture' to me to hear you call them that.

HELEN / Why you ugly beast! What would you have him call us then? Cat and dog?

LORD F / By no means, miss. For that would sound ten times more like man and wife.

TOBIAS / A fine rogue this is to come a-wooing!

NURSE / A fine rogue indeed, upon my soul! Ha ha!

[*TUMMOUS* RE-ENTERS]

TUMMOUS / Sir, there are some gentlemen arrived who claim to be guests of Lord… "Fro'tham"?

CHUMLEY / (*low to Tom*) 'S'truth, Tom, what will you do now?

LORD F / Now, Sir Tobias, here at last are witnesses who I believe cannot all be corrupted.

TOBIAS / Quiet, man!
(*to Tummous*) Put them in the hall for now.

[*TUMMOUS* EXITS]

TOM / (*low to Lovelace and Chumley*) Egad, gentlemen, the truth will out now.

LOVELACE / (*low to Tom*) Confess. Confess all. We'll stand by you.

LORD F / Sir Tobias, I insist on your calling evidence for both sides, and if I do not prove that fellow an imposter…

TOM / ...Brother, I will save you the trouble.
-Sir Tobias, I am a gentleman, and I flatter myself, a man of sound character, and it is also with great pride that I assure you I am not his lordship.

TOBIAS / Oons! -- What is this? -- An imposter? -- A cheat? -- Fire and faggots, sir! If you are not Lord Front-bottom, who the devil are you?

TOM / Sir, the better part of me is your son-in-law, the worst part is the brother of that noble fool of a peer.

LORD F / Impudent to the last, Gad dem me!

TOBIAS / My son-in-law? Not yet, thank God!

TOM / Begging your pardon, sir, but thanks to the goodness of your chaplain and the kind services of this good woman earlier...

TOBIAS / What!

JOHNSON / (*lying through his teeth*) 'Tis true indeed, sir. I gave your daughter away, and Mrs Nurse was the witness, (*now gaining confidence*) the bridesmaid wore beige and gave a wonderful organ recital before the blushing bride and handsome...

TOBIAS / (*interrupting*) I'll give you a wonderful black eye if you don't hold your tongue!

JOHNSON / (*to Tom*) I'll ready the horses, sir.

[**JOHNSON** EXITS HURRIEDLY, **TUMMOUS** STEPS BACK IN AS IF TO SEE WHAT THE COMMOTION IS]

TOBIAS / Nurse? How did all this happen?! Tell me this isn't so!

NURSE / Alas, your honour, forgive me. I have been foolishly deceived in this business, just as you have. Your worship knows that had the wedding breakfast been ready you would have married her with your own hands.

TOBIAS / But for what reason did you do all this without informing me?

Act V Scene II. That Evening In Muddy Moat Hall

[*NURSE* GESTICULATES IN ANSWER AND AS IF BY WAY OF EXPLANATION A COIN OR TWO FALLS FROM HER CLOTHING]

NURSE / Oh, sir, if you had only seen how the poor thing begged and pleaded and clung and entwined her way round me like ivy on an old stone wall, you would say I, who nursed her and reared her, would have had a heart of stone had I refused her.

TOBIAS / Oons! I shall go mad! Untie my lord there, you scoundrels!

LORD F / Yes, and be quick about it, I am looking forward to congratulating 'his honour' on his new son-in-law, once I have a little more freedom to address him with.

[*TUMMOUS* STARTS TO UNTIE *LORD F*]

HELEN / By golly, now I don't know which is to be my husband. Do I have to marry this lord too?

NURSE / Oh no, you can't marry two husbands, cherub.

HELEN / Why not? It sounds more interesting than just one. And anyway, you've had three husbands, nurse, so you can't talk.

NURSE / Aye, but not at the same time, dear.

TOBIAS / Hold your tongue, meddling woman! You are the cause of this predicament. I'll be dealing with you later! Now get out of my sight!

[EXIT *NURSE* SOBBING, A COIN OR TWO DROP AS SHE FLEES]

LOVELACE / Come, come, Sir Tobias. A man of your understanding must perceive that an affair of this kind is not mended by anger and reproaches.

TOBIAS / I don't know who you are, sir, or who anyone is anymore, but one thing I do know, you have all come here thinking you can trick me out of a daughter!

CHUMLEY / Sir Tobias, upon my honour as a military man, you are only tricked into a son-in-law you can be proud of. Tom, here is as honest and caring a fellow as ever lived and breathed, whereas the lord here...

TOBIAS / ...IS a lord I now find!

LOVELACE / That he is, though one best kept as far as possible from one's nearest and dearest lest he try to molest them before your very face! Be reasonable, old boy, fate has dealt you a lucky hand, forgive and forget...

TOBIAS / ...NEVER! The hussy! Not when I – and her poor, dear, departed mother too - had our hearts set on getting her a title!

LORD F / Well, now I am untied, Sir Tobias, it gives me opportunity to thank you for the very extraordinary reception I have been met with in this damned pathetic excuse for a mansion you have. Of all the bumpkins and blockheads I have ever had the misfortune to meet, you are the most obstinate, ignorant and ill-mannered, - strike me ugly!

TOBIAS / What's this? You are both rogues alike!

LORD F / No, Sir Tobias, you will find to your unspeakable mortification that I am the real Lord Fro'tham, - and it is FROTH'AM, not FRONT-BOTTOM! – a lord who, to his utmost 'harror', now realizes he was about to disgrace himself in an alliance with a clod.

TOBIAS / A clod? How dare you sir!

LORD F / And now I find I am saved from eternal misfortune since you, in all your unfathomable wisdom, have chosen to match your wretch of a girl to that beggar of a younger brother of mine, whose title deeds let it be known, would not even fill a tobacco tin. May they both beg on the streets with my blessing.

TOBIAS / Poppy cock! I assure you, sir, I could give them as good an allowance as your lordship, any day.

Act V Scene II. That Evening In Muddy Moat Hall

LORD F / Aye, but you won't. For that would mean acting like a Christian instead of the ill-educated savage you obviously are! - Strap my vitals!

TOBIAS / A savage! Curses and abominations, you make me furious! Six more words from you, sir, and I will forgive and forget what they have done and double their yearly allowance. Let that show you how Christian I can be!

LOVELACE / And be blessed for doing so!

LORD F / Him be blessed? Only if he marries her to one of his pigs, keeping up the family tradition!

TOBIAS / I warn you, sir! I am within one breath of feeding you to the pigs and serving you up stuffed as their wedding banquet!

AMANDA / Good Sir Tobias, restrain yourself, the man is an ass and not worth boiling your blood over. Surely a man as wise and worldly as yourself cannot help but see the better choice has been made for you in this matter. All you need do, sir, is give your consent. They plainly love each other dearly.

SOPHIA / Oh yes, sir. I am such a romantic fool in these things, I couldn't abide seeing two people who didn't love each other forced into marrying.

AMANDA / (*looking accusingly at Sophia*) Unless one of them was exceedingly wealthy and not long for this world.

SOPHIA / (*surprised*) Amanda?

AMANDA / (*to Sir Tobias*) You were young once yourself, sir, surely your daughter's happiness is more important than a title. Character is so much more beautiful an asset in my eyes, it can be admired from afar, (*accusingly*) isn't that so, husband? (*seductively*) ...and may I say, sir, you have it in abundance. You must reconsider.

TOBIAS / I have? Well then... -But first, see... - no, THROW that sneering lord out. Let me have my revenge on someone at least. As to whether I am a savage or not, look here, Lord ARSE-BOTTOM, see, I join their hands. And perhaps later when I am in better humour I may even go as far as giving them my blessing, since your 'Lordship' has deemed so kind as to provide the merriment for this evening.

CHUMLEY / Nobly done, Sir Tobias! We shall see you dance at your grandson's christening yet!

HELEN / By golly, I am confused. I don't understand any of this! Am I not to be a lady after all? Just plain old Mrs... what is my husband's name?

LORD F / Squire Nobody!

HELEN / Squire is he? - - Well I suppose that's better than nothing.

LORD F / I'll show you people it's not possible to ignore a man of my quality.
(*sarcastic*) My dear 'Lord Tam'. I wish you happiness and joy in marrying such a fine young '*lady*', one whose rare lack of breeding and education is matched only by her paucity of decorum - split my windpipe!

HELEN / By golly, husband, break his bones if he calls me names!

TOM / Your lordship may greet the occasion if he so wishes with bitterness, but I shall celebrate it, pending my father-in-law's approval of course, with this fine lady and three thousand pounds a year. I do hope the wine you provided for this evening is of suitable quality for a couple of such wealth.

LORD F / (*smarmily*) I bid you fond farewell, 'Tam'. - May I be the first to wish the conniving couple every success in the gutter having speedily consumed their ill-gotten fortune.
-Ladies, do excuse me, I would kiss your hands, but I fear I may catch something.
-Sir Tobias, I shall now vacate this monstrosity of a hovel while I still have the use of my arms. I shall forever remember you as the horrid savage you are, - Ged dem me!

Act V Scene II. That Evening In Muddy Moat Hall

[*LORD F* LEAVES, SLAMMING THE DOOR. DISTANT MUSIC IS HEARD STARTING AS THE MUSICIANS OUTSIDE SPOT *LORD F* COMING OUT. HE GIVES AN INDISTINCT OATH, AND THE MUSIC GRINDS TO A HALT.]

TOBIAS / By heavens, it's a good thing he's gone. One more minute and he would have provoked me into handing down some mischief with my fists, so help me! Well, if that is a lord, I think Miss Helen has luck on her side in all truth.

CHUMLEY / She has indeed, Sir Tobias. I heard violins – I do believe his lordship arranged and paid for them, ha, ha.

AMANDA / Oh, a dance and a bottle of wine, or perhaps something a little more lively and exciting, Sir Tobias, in celebration? (*taking his arm to effect the seduction*) Champagne perhaps?

[THE ORCHESTRA STARTS UP AGAIN WITH DANCING MUSIC]

TOBIAS / I had forgotten the company outside. Well — let's be merry then, eh? A dance and a drink, what? Before St George, you can't say I do things by halves.
My son-in-law looks a hearty rogue, so we'll make a night of it, and which of these ladies will be this old man's partner in a dance, eh?

SOPHIA / Old? Not at all, you are in your prime. A most desirable age.

TOBIAS / I am? Goodness, I don't know how I came to be in such good humour. I was resigned to the likes of Dame Cummins for dance company before tonight.

LOVELACE / Oh yes, Dame Cummins, the main protagonist in all this. Strange, being the town matchmaker she never married herself.

AMANDA / Some ladies I think you'll find, dearest, have different inclinations.

LOVELACE / (*taken aback*) Inclinations?

SOPHIA / (*impressed*) My, my, Amanda, you have learnt well.

[*SOPHIA* JOINS *AMANDA* AND LINKS THE OTHER ARM OF *TOBIAS*]

SOPHIA / (*silky seduction, competing for Tobias' attention*) Well, Sir Tobias, 'my friend' and I, I am sure, can be most entertaining company for such a noble gentleman as yourself. We will endeavour to keep your spirit up. I see we have raised a smile already, the night is young, let us see if we can improve on that shall we?

TOBIAS / Egads, ladies, with all my heart I approve, though I am the biggest fool in this whole story it seems.

AMANDA / Not at all. You have made a noble gesture and are entitled to our attentions. The Colonel and my husband here I am sure would be more than happy to relate the plot of your daughter's marriage - and his lordship's mortification - to your new guests, allowing us ladies the freedom to entertain you.
(*to Lovelace*) Isn't that right, dearest?

LOVELACE / (*unsure of the change in Amanda*) Yes, right, dearest, we will assist you, of course. And if the tale is judged worthy of repeating we can always invent some finer points along the way, eh, Colonel?

COLONEL / (*hesitant*) Why, yes, yes of course.

AMANDA / Good then it is settled. Come let us all celebrate this happy occasion.

LOVELACE / Come, Colonel. Let us play our part and leave the ladies to play theirs.

COLONEL / Yes. Right. Did you say there was wine?

[*LOVELACE* AND *CHUMLEY* EXIT TOWARDS THE MUSIC]

AMANDA / Shall we dance, Toby? You don't mind if we call you Toby do you?

Act V Scene II. That Evening In Muddy Moat Hall

TOBIAS / Not at all, my dear. Such delicate hands you have.

[*AMANDA* AND *SOPHIA* SLOWLY LEAD *SIR TOBIAS* TOWARDS THE DOOR]

SOPHIA / I find it difficult to believe a fine man such as yourself never remarried. Had I mentioned I was a widow? I love being married, a strong man to have and to hold me, keep me warm at night.

TOBIAS / Goodness, I agree heartily, but who would have the likes of me?

SOPHIA / Oh, Toby, any woman in her right mind would want to have you.

AMANDA / Sophia! You have the Colonel!

SOPHIA / Oh, you can amuse yourself with him, Amanda. I've found myself a real man now.

AMANDA / And one not married to someone else.

SOPHIA / Like one of us, Amanda?

AMANDA / I was under the impression both of us were with a married man.

SOPHIA / Who on earth could have told you that nonsense, Amanda?

AMANDA / A married man I overheard earlier.

SOPHIA / Oh, don't believe anything you overhear from married men, Amanda, especially when addressing unmarried women.

AMANDA / As you said Sophia, I have learnt well, and he did offer *me* the first dance, though I would happily settle for the last dance… the sweetest dance of all, eh Toby?

SOPHIA / Tonight he can share us, Amanda. I am sure a big strong man such as Sir Tobias could handle two delicate ladies together.

TOBIAS / I am not at all sure I'm not dreaming, someone pinch me.

SOPHIA / *(exiting)* You must tell us all about yourself, Toby.

AMANDA / Yes, how much did you say you were worth again?

[EXIT *SOPHIA*, *AMANDA* AND *SIR TOBIAS*]

TOM / *(After the departing couple)* As they say, my dear: "All's fair in love and money".

HELEN / Oh no, "Money before business". That's what Nurse always tells the parson.

TOM / Talking of business, I had almost forgotten. It's our wedding night. Let us dance in celebration. Later, I have something for you.

HELEN / Oh no, sir. I think I have something for YOU.

TOM / *(leaning in to kiss her)* Better and better.

[THEY KISS, AS THE FINAL CURTAIN FALLS]

THE END

www.ingramcontent.com/pod-product-compliance
Ingram Content Group UK Ltd.
Pitfield, Milton Keynes, MK11 3LW, UK
UKHW041435180426
11947UKWH00007B/464